The Queen, The Rogue, and The Apprentice

D. T. Gilmour

For David Armstrong, the first to see the stories that bubbled within.

For Sian, a long-awaited reward for your patience.

The Queen

Chapter I

Wind whistled in her ears. The beast beneath her galloped, adjusting to every twitch and tug of the reins. Trunks passed in a blur; occasionally, a startled squawk chased after them, but not until she had been carried far from the offended creature.

'Faster,' she urged, leaning closer to his neck. She held herself over the saddle, legs burning as she reacted to every lurch and tilt, balancing her weight on the stirrups. Together, they raced through the woodland, the horse having relented control long ago. Áxil had given himself up to trust, simply moving to the instructions of his rider. She was his brain, he her body.

With every tree that fizzed by, another replaced it, sparing her little time to think. Act and react .

The thunder of hooves kept time with her heart, her usual concern for Áxil's wellbeing left at the stable. Despite the speed, she was not reckless. Every movement was calculated, predicted, accounted for. She ducked branches as he soared over fallen trunks, moving more as one being than two, until, like a hawk bursting from a cloud, they broke from the trees. She grinned from the exhilaration, settling herself back into the saddle and recovering her breath as she pulled him to a gradual halt.

Around them, trees had fallen away into open land. Sparse plains rolled until hills swept up, clambering higher into the haunches of the O'Pasos. She cocked her head back, drawing in great breaths of morning air, laughing as she recovered. *How long has it been?* she wondered, patting Áxil on the neck as she stared to the mountain range. 'One day,' she promised. 'Maybe a wedding, or the birth of an heir. Perhaps a princess awaits somewhere beyond the Hackles.' She knew it to be fanciful. The coastal kingdom of Duna had borne only princes, but she let her imagination entertain her, as though the alliance between the northern powers had not dissolved several summers ago.

The sting of a cold wind returned her to the plains, and she turned Áxil southward to face her own kingdom. Save for the isolated farms that occupied the lands beyond Corazin, the road was empty. Few travellers ventured farther north this close to the winter months, with many choosing to retreat to the southern cities until spring. In the pale morning light, the city was a splendour that she rarely saw: its outer walls sprouting from a low hill, stretching high to the wisps of cloud above. Beyond, the inner walls could be seen, and if she squinted, the very tops of the palace could be glimpsed reflecting in the sunlight.

Despite her admiration for the city, she wondered if it was ever somewhere she would call home. After nearly twenty years trapped inside the walls, she doubted it. Dessius had never understood her yearning to escape, to be free of the looming stone and constant gaggle of noise; it was what he had most loved about the city. Yet, he had been loath to let her free of his confines, and seldom was she at the liberty to roam as she was now. After one occasion in her younger years, when she had snuck out similarly to how she had that morning, he had insisted on providing a space for his queen to relax and seek freedom from the demands of palace life. He had had the garden built like the city around it: tall and over-powering. Aromas competed for her attention and flowers grew unnaturally. He could not seem to understand that it was the natural freedom that she craved, to simply stand as an insignificant speck in an open expanse.

There was one spot in the garden that she had decided was appropriate for what she sought. It was concealed from the walls, hidden behind the drooping branches of the trees, offering a welcoming shade in the summer months. Here, she could almost trick herself into thinking she had escaped, that she had been transported to some place far from Corazin, until the braying of a horse or some other commotion from beyond the walls located her back to her gardens.

Movement drew her eyes from the city. Breaking free from the road, a cloud of dust billowed its way towards her. 'I suppose we were longer than I thought, hey, Áxil?' she said, though guilt eluded her. She tapped her heels to his flanks, letting her body rock and sway with the horse's movements. Regret tickled at her, and she realised her guard would not be so easy to slip for a time. She sighed but decided the morning's escapade had been worth it.

As the figure neared, she strained her eyes to recognise who it was that approached. Despite the colours of his horse's crinet, she couldn't help the unease that gnawed at her stomach. *They have no business north of the city,* she reminded herself.

Her shoulders relaxed when she saw it was Theon: a polite palace guard she had fleetingly spoken to on a few occasions. She lifted her chin, straightened her back, and forced her hair into order. 'Queen Serana,' he heralded. 'You're missed in the palace. Reports were that you'd taken your horse and fled.' He sidled next to her, but she did not slow. He wheeled his horse about and caught up to her.

'Can a queen not ride her horse when she wishes?'

'But, Your Grace,' he said. 'There are those who would seek to cause you harm. Is this wise?'

She raised an eyebrow. 'Are you to say what your queen may or may not do, Theon? Have you taken on the role of my private council?' She regarded him a moment, yet he was wise to speak no more. 'You step too far. Unless, of course, you wish to spend the winter sharpening blades and mucking out the stables.'

He paled. 'No, Your Highness. Never. I only think for your safety, that's all.'

'Your concern is appreciated, but Áxil here would keep me far safer than any man trained with a blade.' She patted the horse affectionately. 'Besides, if it is what Fate has destined, there is no score of men that could have any influence on the matter.'

Theon chewed his lip for a moment. 'Perhaps, but might I still escort you back to Corazin, Your Grace? I fear to think what Captain Islo would do should he discover I let my queen return alone, especially after recent events.'

She grimaced. 'I would share your fears. You may ride ahead, Theon.'

'My thanks, Queen Serana. We shall be swift.'

Once returned to the road, Serana lifted her shawl to keep plumes of dust from drying her throat. The road grew steadily busier as they approached. The small village that dwelled in the shadow of Corazin was beginning to stir, and vacant eyes swept past them, scarcely noticing their passing. She smiled to herself. If only life could be so simple. She would shirk the royal halls and escape to a tamer life. She knew, though, she had no appetite for the labour, nor the skills. She was armed for court, and few could wield whispers and parchment like she.

Besides, she thought, *the people need to be ruled. Fate has chosen my son, and so by him I stand.* It was sooner than she had hoped—he was little more than a boy—but she could not say she mourned the loss of her husband. Perhaps once, many summers ago, she would have grieved him, but of more recent seasons, romance had crumbled to duty and bitter tolerance. The king had paid her little interest, dealing with few others than whores and wine, letting the council run the kingdom as they saw fit. It would have suited her fine, had he not been so conspicuous about it; the whispers and glances were what bothered her, and had the man known subtlety, she might have turned a blind eye. Instead, she was sniggered at more than the court fool.

Theon slowed once they were beyond the village, nothing but dust and rocks between them and the city gates. 'My queen, might I ask what you were doing so far from the city at such an hour?'

'I thought you were riding ahead,' she said sternly.

'Apologies, Your Grace. My tongue knows little restraint.' He nudged his gelding forward, but she followed, staying close to his shoulder.

'Does it surprise you that a wife might seek solitude in the wake of her beloved's death?'

'No, Your Grace, but were the palace gardens so unsuitable?'

She smirked. 'A widow might wish to mourn in peace, Theon. The gardens provide little solace from the prying eyes and keen ears of those who might exploit weakness. The eyes and ears of songbirds are more sympathetic.'

'I apologise, Your Highness. I did not intend to pry, myself.'

They rode in silence for a while before Serana drew level with the man. 'Do you have a wife, Theon? One who bears your heart?'

He kept his eyes ahead, but she saw his jaw tighten. 'I'm married to the crown, my queen. I cannot take a wife if I would die for another.'

'Come now,' she scoffed, 'there must be a maid. I know the hearts of men, and if not their heart, I know men. Madam Sorrell's would not be full every evening if I did not.'

Theon flushed. 'Your Grace, I'd ask we do not speak of such things.'

She grinned behind her shawl. 'Very well, but you have not escaped my question.'

He squirmed for a moment before his shoulders fell. 'There is a maid, Your Highness.'

'Ah, I was not wrong. What is her name? Tell me about her.'

'Dhalia, Your Grace. She's the most beautiful woman in the city, aside from yourself, of course.'

'Enough flattery. You have already lied to your queen, don't give me another reason to tell your captain that you spoke to me of brothels and other uncomely topics.'

He glanced to her from the corner of his eye, swallowing hastily. 'I beg your pardon, Your Grace. She—she's a serving girl at an inn, not far from the eastern gate. She has hair as dark as soot and a smile like sunshine on a summer's morning.'

'And you have courted her?'

'I am a king's man, Your Grace. I have not.'

Serana smiled sympathetically. 'You are a good man, Theon.'

As they approached the gates and into the shadow of the walls, she let Theon pull ahead as she lowered her shawl. She nodded to the guards who stood with backs straight on either side of the gate, unmoving aside from their eyes. Within the walls, the city was already awake and bustling. Merchants crossed paths, moving wares and setting up stalls. Shutters were being pinned open and the steady rhythm of a smith's hammer welcomed them.

A tray of baked pastries walked ahead, not noticing the others who had parted to allow the passage of horses. 'Make way for the queen,' Theon barked.

The tray jolted, spilling its contents. The man caught a loaf of bread as he stumbled, losing the rest to the trodden-down earth. Theon circled the baker. 'Have you lost your hearing, man? The queen approaches. Make way!' People stalled in their tracks to watch on.

The man dropped to his knees, his head bowed. 'A-a thousand pardons, Your Highness. I was half asleep. It's my daughter, you see. She's just a babe, and she keeps us—'

'The queen does not want to hear your excuses,' Theon sneered. 'Stand aside, or you'll have to learn to knead bread without thumbs.'

The man paled, and lifted a quivering hand to present Serana with the single loaf he had saved. 'Please, take this by way of apology. I didn't mean to stall my queen.'

Serana drew Áxil before the man. 'Rise, baker. What is your name?'

'Portland, Your Highness.'

'And how much has my presence cost you, here?'

'N-nothing, Your Grace. It is an honour to share your presence.'

'Nonsense. I will not have my people falling upon hard ground when times are already harsh.' She looked up to Theon, who watched the gathering crowd warily. 'How much would this have made Mr Portland, here.'

'I can only guess, Your Grace, but no more than a gold piece. A dozen silvers, perhaps.'

She dipped a hand into her jerkin. 'Hold out your hand, Mister Portland.' His hand shook as he held his palm up to her, head still bowed. 'I apologise for any inconveniences I have caused you.'

The man's eyes lit up as the weight dropped into his palm. 'But, Your Grace, this is double what I would've made.'

She inclined her head, smiling gently. 'For your troubles.' She tapped her heels to Áxil's flanks and left the man staring after her. Theon clattered behind her, but she only slowed beyond the inner walls.

'So it's as they say,' Theon said, catching up to her. 'You are as gracious as you are beautiful, my queen. I doubt he'll forget that as long as he lives.'

'Perhaps not. The throne could do with more of those in our favour. This rebellion will only be beaten when the people decide it so.'

As they neared the palace, a pair of guards stepped aside, admitting them onto the grounds. They trotted to the stables where Serana swung down from the saddle and patted Áxil on the jaw. He huffed a return of affection just as a stable-boy hurried out from the stalls. 'It is okay, Kile, I will take care of Áxil. It is hardly fair that he cares for me and not I for him. I am sure you have many other tasks this morning.'

He thanked her, but Theon held his horse's reins to the boy. 'Your Grace, I must insist that you accompany me to Captain Islo. He wishes to speak with you.'

'Then he will just have to wait a little longer. If he required my attention so desperately, he would have sought me before I departed this morning. Tell him to report to my chambers, I will attend to him there.'

'Yes, my queen.' Theon said shortly, before bowing and striding towards the barracks. Serana led Áxil into the stable and into his stall. She unsaddled him, removed his bridle and fetched him water and some oats before brushing out his mane and throwing fresh straw about his stall. With a farewell pat, she left the stables and made her way up to the doors of the Great Hall.

Vibrant tapestries hung from the walls, works of pottery and stone welcomed her as servants and maids scuttled from doorways. The high roof made every sound echo, and it was rare to find the hall without a clamour of activity. Everyone that walked past called a greeting, and many of the new servants stopped to bow or curtsey, a gesture she returned with a smile, but it was something Serana still stiffened at. It was one thing to be queen in her city, quite another to be queen in her own home. *I will have to address the new staff and order this crazed behaviour out of them—there is too much work to be done to be wasting time curtseying and bowing to every lord and lady they walk past.*

Doors lined the walls on either side of the hall, leading off into the network of corridors and rooms around the palace. The royal quarters were adjoined at the back of the hall, with two guards standing in front of the doors, waiting to challenge anyone who they deemed not to belong; they were silent as she stepped inside.

The corridors beyond were quieter. A page hurried on ahead of her and turned around a corner before she came to her door. She was just reaching for the handle when she hesitated. It was already open ajar. Easing it open, she let it swing on oiled hinges. A step inside revealed the culprit. A rotund woman, with red cheeks and her hair pulled back in a tail, was bundling Serana's bedding into her arms. When she saw Serana, she started, dropping the linen with a yelp.

'Stop doing that,' she hissed, gathering herself. 'At least clear your throat or scuff your foot. You'll make my heart stop one of these days.'

Serana did not bother to hide her smile. Laila was the easiest person to startle in Corazin, intentionally or otherwise.

'I'm glad to see you're safe, though,' she continued, bending over to pick up the linen. 'Captain Islo said—'

'Yes, yes. Leave that where it is. I am expecting him shortly and I do not intend to meet him in riding attire.'

'Of course, my queen. Right away.'

Serana scowled at her. 'What have I told you about that?'

'About what?' she said, bustling about her, scooping up a discarded nightgown. Serana caught her by the arm.

'Laila, you are my oldest friend. If I had known you were going to start treating me like a queen, I would never have asked you to be my handmaid.'

She smiled guiltily. 'I can't help it. I hear everyone else doing it around here, and, well, I just follow suit.'

'If I hear it again, I'll have you scrubbing dishes for a week.'

'Is that supposed to be worse than scrubbing your chamber pot?' she smirked, and with that, they were teenage girls again, grinning over some daft joke. 'Come on, before the captain sees you in your indecency.'

'He wouldn't look twice,' Serana said, the corner of her mouth lifting. 'Now, if I were Dessius, then he would never take his eyes off of me.'

The two women sputtered out giggles. 'You know,' Laila said, slipping a jerkin and undershirt from Serana's shoulders, 'I heard that he purposefully set a recruit against a better swordsman. All so that when he got beaten, Islo could take him to the infirmary himself. One of the nurses even said that he stayed by the recruit's side for most of the day, telling him war stories and tales of his own adventures.'

Serana raised her eyebrow. 'Is that it? He used to refuse to let the king use the baths on his own. What if he were attacked? Much better to have two nude men against an attacker than one.' The fits of giggles continued as Laila helped Serana into a black gown with laced grey hems along the sleeve. These were the moments she missed most, where she could relax and not worry at how her words might be twisted. Laila was a confidante as much as a handmaid, and that made her one of the most important people in the city to her. *Pretences must be sustained,* she thought, composing herself once more.

She looked down at the gown that spilled over her hips. Wearing such gloomy clothing brought her mood to match it, though who she was fooling with it, she was unsure. It was only as Laila stood over her shoulder, brushing her hair out, that a knock come from the door.

Serana took a deep breath and let it out slowly, returning to the role of Queen of Corazin. 'Enter,' Serana called sharply.

The door opened to admit a broad-chested man. He wore padded leather and stiff boots. His neatly trimmed hair was as uniform as his clothes, the blazon of Corazin—a burning heart set against a mountain background—embroidered onto his chest. He bowed deeply. 'My queen.'

'Captain,' she said.

'You were absent from this morning's assembly.'

'It appears so.'

He narrowed his eyes. 'Where were you?'

'Getting some air.'

'Your Grace,' he said stiffly. 'So soon after the assassination, do you really think it a good idea for you to go galloping across the countryside?'

Serana flew to her feet, her hair spilling from Laila's hand. 'Watch your tongue, Captain. I have had enough of people assuming they can tell me what I can and cannot do, never mind where I can and cannot go. This is my kingdom. I am free to roam it.'

'This might be your kingdom, but there are those who seek to snatch it from you.'

'Let them try,' she snapped. 'I am not as foolish as my husband. Wine will not dull my wits, nor will I let strangers into my private chambers.'

The captain flushed but refused to yield. 'My queen, not even you can hope to stand against a Maxia assassin. Magic is not as easily defended against as a blade.'

'And what would you suggest? If you hadn't noticed, the court Maxia was murdered that night, too, along with the strongest guards in the city. If I am not safe in my own home, I am safe nowhere.'

The captain bristled, choosing his words with care. 'Let us do our jobs, Your Grace. Reconsider having guards on your door, men to shadow you.' Serana glared at him, refusing to enter into this argument again.

'Fine,' he snapped, 'but if you send another soldier to me rejecting my own orders and relaying that you demand I meet you in your quarters, I should very well leave you and this city to your Fate.'

She sighed. It was an idle threat, but there was little use in making an enemy without cause. Serana composed herself and settled back into her chair as Laila resumed her task. 'You are right, captain. You have my apologies. I will reconsider having men on my door, but I will not have them follow me like a puppy after its mother. What kind of a message will it send if the queen is walking with an armed guard everywhere she goes?'

'That the queen values her life.'

'Or that she is frightened by the threats not directed at her. Walking on my own sends a stronger message to our enemies than if I were seen hiding behind the palace guard.'

'You would be seen as vulnerable, Your Highness.'

Serana pursed her lips. 'I will think on it, Captain.'

His shoulders relaxed and he seated himself opposite. 'I only want what is best for you, Your Grace. What would happen if we were to lose you? What would Prince Raiden do without his mother?'

Her lips thinned, but she remained silent.

'He is but a boy, Your Majesty. The council do not think he has what it takes to rule, nor do the people. He needs you. As does your kingdom.'

She spoke through tight lips. "Why are you here, Islo?'

His eyes flicked to Laila. 'It's best spoken of alone.'

Serana lifted a hand. 'We are alone. Laila does not hear words not spoken to her.'

He narrowed his eyes, knitting his fingers on his lap. 'Our spies report unrest among the rebels. Fights break out among their troops. Many are homesick. If we take them by surprise, I believe many will flee. I suggest we make the first move.'

'You have discussed this with the council?'

He shook his head. 'No, Your Grace. This is my counsel and mine alone. I do not wish the council's influence on matters that are not yet afoot.'

She nodded, appreciating the gesture. The council would twist and struggle against any firm action, but kindling an idea in private gave her time to prepare a counter against the council's arguments and schemes. 'So, how many?'

'At least a thousand. Probably more.'

'Then we do nothing.' She rose to her feet and walked to a dresser, picking at a tray of pastries.

'Nothing?' he said, standing after her.

'Nothing. They are small. We have strong walls and have not been provoked. If we act, it will not be seen as retaliation, but rather an act of brutality on innocent people.'

'They are responsible for the death of the king,' he said incredulously. 'To not act is to tie the knot around our own necks.'

'You have proof that my husband was killed by these rebels?'

He glared at her. 'You cannot just sit idly. Your people will suffer for it.'

Serana shrugged. 'You said it yourself, they grow restless. We will not act, only react. Darrius is not the kind of man to do things without making a show of it. We will play our hand when he does. If he shows himself at our gates, he should not be harmed.'

Captain Islo's cheeks assumed a red tinge and a vein on his forehead bulged slightly. She looked at it, wondering if it were possible for him to get angry enough for it to burst. 'The king would have ill-advised this.'

'I am not the king,' she said, 'and a good thing, too. He is dead. I am not. Do as you are commanded, Captain, otherwise I will find a more obedient man for the title.' She kept an eye on the vein, yet, to her disappointment, it remained intact. 'If that is all, I would be alone now.'

He bowed sharply and swung the door shut after him. Serana breathed out and threw herself onto her unmade bed.

'Are you okay?' Laila was watching her, a bemused smile on her lips.

'Do I get a choice?'

'Perhaps. You're the most powerful woman in the kingdom. You can do whatever you want.'

She sighed. 'I'd rather someone else did the thinking for me.'

Laila held her hands up. 'Don't look at me. I'm only here to clean your clothes and scrub your floors.' They fell silent for a moment, and Laila went about tidying the rest of the room, leaving the linen by the door.

'Islo is right,' Serana said glumly. 'Sitting idle will only tempt action, and without knowing what they are planning, we cannot plan ourselves.'

'Then why didn't you say anything?'

'Soldiers are too loud, too obvious. Some things need a more delicate hand....' She stood, straightened her clothes, and stepped towards the door. 'I am going to the kennels. Send no one unless Darrius himself is knocking at the gates.'

Chapter II

Serana approached the kennels, vacantly nodding and smiling to those she passed. Her mother had taught her that a good queen knows the name of every servant in the palace, and at first, she had done her best to learn everyone's name. It was not until the seasons turned and came again that she realised it was a never-ending, near-impossible task. Workers came and left; maids and cooks moved with the seasons. In winter, there was less work to be done with fewer visitors; the gardens could not be tended under blankets of snow, and any construction must be finished before the ice made any work too hazardous. Those who remained were often those who called Corazin home, or those who hoped it would be for winter, at least.

The door to the kennels hung open, and hurtling from the confines of the building came a small, white terricr came, followed by a scruffy haired boy. 'You get back 'ere, damned mutt.' The dog glanced over its shoulder, tongue lolling as it bounded this way and that, finding a giddy joy in eluding its young master. As the dog approached, Serana bent down and scooped it into the air, legs still running in confusion.

'Bloody hound,' the boy said, jogging over. 'Never does as it's told. If I were Mr Kerrick I'd—' He faltered when he looked up to see who it was that had captured his escapee. He ducked his head immediately, cheeks rushing to a deep red. 'My apologies, Queen Serana. Didn't know it was you.'

She smiled kindly, returning the dog. 'It is quite alright, Tom. Though I think you and I both know that Mr Kerrick would care for this dog and train him just as he has the others.'

'Yes, Your Grace.' He ducked his head again, wrestling with the small dog.

'Speaking of the man, do you know where I can find him?'

'With Hila, Your Grace. Gave birth to pups, she did.'

She nodded to Tom and he hurried ahead of her, wrestling to keep a hold on the dog. Serana had always been fond of the kennels. When she had first been married to Dessius, this was where she would go, seeking reprieve from the false smiles and courteous invitations. The dogs knew not her name or what her title meant, only that she gave them a fuss, and occasionally a sliver of dried meat.

Inside, the air was musty. Stalls held packs of dogs, some larger than others, all of them rising at her scent to greet her. She paused to lean over a door and scratch behind the ear of one of the brown mutts they took on hunts. Behind its wagging tail, others swished patiently, not pushing past the alpha for attention, instead hoping that they, too, might get some form of attention.

'Why are people not like you?' she asked quietly. Many laughed at those who spoke to animals, but she had always believed that, whilst they could not understand her words, they could understand the emotion within them. 'There's no politics under this roof, hey, Cazdor? Just plain old hierarchy. If only the council could be as easily swayed by food and a scratched belly.' She shook her head with a chuckle before making her way to the opposite end of the kennel. In the last stall, a scrawny man leaned over a bitch, her pups yipping softly. Several grey hairs had escaped the knot in his hair, but he ignored them, giving the dog his entire attention. It had been a long night for both of them.

'How does she fare?'

'Not well,' he said gruffly, not looking up. 'But she's survived worse. She'll do.' He climbed slowly to his feet, stretching his hunched back as he walked to the stall door. He shut it behind him, gnarled hands deftly sliding a bolt across. 'To what do I owe the honour?'

She met his eyes, grey and withered, yet sharp. 'A dog in the village has fallen down the well.'

His jaw tightened, but acknowledgement came from his eyes. 'Follow me, then.'

They walked back along the stalls, Kerrick dropping the occasional pat on the head to a dog or tidying away a piece of leather. He picked up several leashes and hung them by the doors, instructing Tom as he went. It was a slow walk, as though he struggled with every step, but she did not press nor harry him; Kerrick was not a man to be rushed. Outside, they turned around the side of the building and up a set of stairs to his chambers.

When Kerrick had been promoted to his station of beast-master, he had been offered quarters within the palace, but he had refused, preferring to be close to his animals. At first, the thought had been preposterous. 'A man should seek time away from his labour,' Dessius had said, so they had a room prepared and his hearth lit every night. It was only when they had found the room empty again and the man curled on a bed of straw next to a sick hound that they relented. Serana had once asked him why.

'These animals are my family,' he had said. 'You would not leave a child unattended during the night, nor will I. The leader of a pack must be with his pack, otherwise they will not see him as such.' She had thought his words curious but found no argument against it.

At the top of the steps, a door gave way to a sparse, boxed room. A narrow writing desk sat a quill and papers. The hearth was cold and had not been swept in many nights; his bed was a bundle of blankets and furs. He pulled a seat from his work bench, shuffling tools aside, before offering it to Serana.

'It has been many months since you asked this of me,' he said, scratching the stubble on his chin.

'The summer has been kind to our kingdom. Are you surprised by my visit?'

He grunted and sat on the edge of his bed. 'I had expected you sooner, though I do not know what I can offer. The assassins were Maxia. They moved, killed, and covered their tracks with magic. My skills will not help you here, Your Grace.

Serana smiled softly. 'I know, Kerrick. I would ask of you something more.'

'Oh?' he raised an eyebrow.

'I would ask that you leave the kennels for a time. That you visit the village to the south.'

'You would ask me to leave my family?'

'Only for a time. You have taken your apprentices for many seasons. Is it not time they were tested?'

His eyes sparkled, but his voice remained gruff. 'What do you ask of me, my queen? To watch and listen, I presume?'

'Indeed.'

'Would there be anything more?'

'Identify Darrius' strongest supporters. Spread unease among the men there—doubt and illness, too. They grow restless, and it should take little to send them snapping at each other.' She sighed and rested against the back of her chair. 'Many will grow bored and leave, others will wait no longer, seeking to undermine those who lead them. Once Darrius and his men approach with an offer, we will invite them as our esteemed guests and do away with his supporters beyond our walls, letting his generals fall ill to poor humour and too much drink. Once a deal is settled, Darrius will return to find his forces no longer there.'

Kerrick shook his head with a smile. 'I wonder what the kingdom would look like were you not here all these years, Your Grace.'

'Smoke and ashes, I imagine.'

'And what of you? What is to be done here?'

Serana hesitated, before closing her eyes. 'If only I knew. Raiden is not yet fit to rule, but I fear the council will seize control of him. They will be loath to relinquish the power they amassed under Dessius.'

The old man nodded slowly, brooding on the thought. 'Keep him close, Your Grace. Teach him to fight as you do, and perhaps there may still be fruitful years ahead.' He paused for a while, picking at a callous on his finger. 'Forgive me, Your Highness, but I wonder why you shy from the role of regent. Raiden would surely learn—'

'It would not be fitting,' she cut him off. 'I am an outlander to these people. Whilst my presence here is tolerated, I do not think the people would take kindly to being ruled by me. No, Raiden must ascend to the throne and I will counsel him until he is of age. He will voice my words, and perhaps when he is old enough, he will have learned how to rule well.'

The sound of boots stomping up the steps outside stalled the conversation, quickly followed by a pounding fist on the door. 'Kerrick, get out here at once,' a voice demanded. 'Your wretched dogs—'

'Not now, Rosetta. I am with a guest,' he said politely, glancing between the queen and the door, a grimace in the corner of his mouth. Serana straightened her posture and cursed the woman quietly.

'Please,' the voice sneered as the door was flung open. 'You haven't had a guest in—' She bit the end of her sentence off, dropping a hurried curtsey. 'Your Grace, I— forgive me for being so rude. I had thought—'

'Nonsense.' The queen smiled gently. 'Please, say what you must to the beast-master. Do not let my presence interrupt you.'

The woman flushed and mumbled an excuse about coming back later.

'Not at all. It is a way from the kitchens, and I do not doubt it busy at this hour. Please, do not let the kitchen's strain for your absence be for naught.'

'Ah. Yes, Your Grace. Thank you, Your Grace.' She wrung her hands before her, shifting her weight from foot to foot as she faced Kerrick. 'Master Kerrick, I would ask that you so kindly keep your dogs in the kennels. They scrounge my kitchens for scraps and nip at the girls when they steal them back. The kitchens are no place for foul-smelling beasts.'

Kerrick bowed his head. 'You have my apologies, Rosetta. Dogs can be fickle creatures, especially when it comes to filling their bellies. Spare them a morsel one day, and they will undoubtedly return the next. I will ask the boys to keep a closer eye on them from now on.'

'That'd be appreciated,' she said, backing out of the room and apologising as she did before a final curtsey. They listened to her hurried footsteps disappear down the steps.

'I fear I have caused you strife, Your Highness. I should not have asked you to talk with me here.'

She sighed. 'No doubt you have, but by no will of your own. The gossip of cooks will burn as hot as their fires, I am sure. Perhaps it is better they talk of their queen in the beast-master's quarters than worrying about the rebel forces that wait on our doorstep.' She rose from the seat and led them to the courtyard before the kennels. 'I must begin preparations for Raiden's tuition. You understand your task?'

'I do, my queen.' His eyes flicked to over her shoulder and she followed his gaze to see a page rushing towards her.

'My queen, my queen,' he shouted.

'I am here, Gellow.'

'I have an urgent message for you.'

Serana bristled. *Laila's going to be scrubbing pots for a week.* 'And what is your message?'

'An audience has been called in the Jade Hall, my queen. Your presence is needed.' He hesitated a moment, then added more quietly. 'At once.'

'It was instructed that I only be sought if Darrius were at our gates. Is the traitor at our gates?'

He opened his mouth, then closed it again. He looked as if he wished he could run right back the way he had come. 'No, my queen, but—'

'Then what reason is worthy of breaking such an order?'

The page cowered, speaking timidly. 'Your Grace, Darrius awaits in the palace. I was sent as soon—'

Serana had already set off towards the Jade Hall, wind and the heat of her rage flapping at her gown. *Why did Islo not send someone immediately?*

Chapter III

The doors crashed open. 'What do you think you are doing?'

Faces turned to look as her voice boomed around them. She stormed towards the dais. Mighty pillars lined the pathway from the door to the steps leading up to the throne; a scarlet carpet joined the two. The throne room, named the Jade Hall because of the green stone that the floor and pillars were made of, was host to a collection of nobles and note-worthy names, all stood in a flock at the bottom of the steps. Every pair of eyes turned to watch her advance. Stained-glass windows pooled light in behind the palace guards, one posted between every pillar. Their armour gleamed, long capes flowing over their backs, swords hanging from their hips, ready to be drawn at a moment's notice. More guards stood at the base of the staircase, but her son was the only one that stood higher.

'Ah, my mother has arrived.' He sat languidly on the throne. The crown was sat on a cushion by his feet. 'You took your time, Mother. Were it you who asked of me, I would be scalded like a child.'

Serana glanced at the council, positioned off to the side, smug smiles on their lips and they shared knowing glances. A knot formed in her stomach. Their presence, along with so many nobles, foretold only mischief. Captain Islo stood at the helm of his guard, dressed in full plate armour. She thought she saw his chin dip as she walked to the bottom of the staircase, but she paid him no mind. 'That is because you *are* a child, Raiden.'

'Not anymore,' he said, hooking the crown on a finger. It swayed for a moment, then his snatched it into his grip and lifted it over his head.

'Raiden,' she cautioned, hesitating on the steps. 'It is against the law to wear the crown if you are not king.'

He lowered it onto his head. 'A good thing I am king, then.' It sat askew, not made for him, but for his father. Before a coronation, the crown was usually amended to fit the king-in-waiting, but this was obviously a scheme devised by opportunists, and while the crown may not have fit, upon his brow it rested.

Serana almost stumbled. She turned and looked back at the council members. Their smirks told all. Lucille, Master of Coin, stepped forth, bowing deeply. 'There is more power within the council than you know, Your Grace. You must understand, when we heard of your disappearance this morning, we could only presume that you had been taken, stolen away by the rebel Maxia who had killed the beloved King Dessius. In a time of such turmoil, Corazin needs solidarity, so we presented His Majesty with a choice.'

She swore to herself and turned on Raiden. 'And you took it?'

'The council are not wrong, Mother. The people need a ruler.'

'My child, you are so young.' She rose to the top of the dais, standing before him. 'There is much to learn. Wait. Only for a year, perhaps two. Then you may fully understand what it means to be king.'

A knowing smile crept across his lips. 'They said you would say that. That you lusted after power and sought to keep the throne for yourself.' The pit of snakes grinned at her from the base of the steps. 'You now have a choice, Mother. Stand beside me as your king and offer me counsel, or leave, and in doing so, admit to treason.'

I am too late, she realised. *They have whispered poison in his ear and he has heard their words but not seen the schemes beneath them.* 'I would be honoured to serve you, my king.' She took another step closer, and in a voice only he could hear, said, 'but do not forget that I am your mother, and I have as much duty in that as your advisor.'

He grunted, shrugging off any acknowledgment. When she took her place by his side, he spoke again, addressing those below. They clustered at the base of the stairs, staring eagerly to him. 'It is time for my first act as king: to rid us of the wolves who howl on our doorstep, ready to strike at any moment and snatch the life we have worked so hard to build.'

Serana leaned forward, whispering in his ear. 'What are you to do, Raiden? I was told Darrius is in the palace.'

The king smiled and raised his voice. 'Bring him in.' The doors at the end of the hall swung open, and in marched a muscular man with a thick beard and shaggy black hair. He walked with a confidence, even in the hall of his enemies. A lone guard, leaning a broadsword on his shoulder, strode at his side. Six palace guards escorted them: a guard of honour, some would say, though Serana would have given it another name.

As they approached, Raiden spoke in a low voice, not taking his eyes from the small procession. 'Whilst we awaited your arrival, he was given time to make himself presentable. I am told the cells suit him rather well.'

The nobles parted, murmuring to each other. They eyed Darrius as though he were a viper and drawing his attention might lead to a strike. His step never faltered as the crowd parted for him, and Serana thought he would have continued up the steps had Captain Islo and another guard not blocked his path.

Raiden stayed sat on the throne. 'Greetings, Uncle. The pleasure is mine.'

He ignored him and faced the queen instead. 'Serana, you let your child run away with fantasy. Have you taught him no manners?'

'Uncle,' Raiden shook his head. 'I am not the boy you knew. I am your king, thus you will treat me so.' He climbed to his feet and stood at the top of the steps, looking down on them. 'Well? I am your king,' he repeated. 'Before your king, do you not bow?' There was a shuffle of movement as the gathering stood, unsure of whom he addressed. 'Guards, the last man or woman to be standing will have their head removed.'

'Raiden,' Serana hissed, but her voice was lost to the sound of bodies dropping to their knees, heads bowed. Darrius and his guard remained standing.

'Uncle, did you not hear me? You bow before your king.'

'You are no king of mine,' he spat.

'Yet, you will kneel all the same.' He looked to one of the six guards who recognised the command. He spun and plunged a mail-clad fist into his stomach. Darrius crumpled, groaning as he did so. Rough hands forced him to his knees, holding him there. Darrius' own guard made to move, but the cold touch of a blade against the back of his neck stilled him.

'Good,' Raiden purred. 'Now, a king is only as good as his word, and my, oh, my. I'm sorry, Uncle. It appears your guard is the last man standing.'

Without another word, the guard lifted the knife away from the base of his skull and plunged the knife into his neck. Serana gasped, just as the dignitaries did. A woman shrieked. The man gurgled, clasped at his throat, then looked at his hands as though shocked at the sight of blood. He fell just after, broadsword clattering to the stone floor. Breathless silence hung in the room.

'Raiden,' Serana started in a hushed voice, 'this is enough.'

He raised a hand to silence her. 'You are right, Mother,' he said, walking down several steps, keeping an eye on Darrius, 'and this is the end. Tell me, Uncle. Why are you here?'

He glanced behind him, the pool of blood still growing. He licked his lips but spoke clearly. 'I am here to return the crown to the people. It's time they ruled themselves.'

'Is it? Well, the crown is right here. Come and retrieve it for them, please.' He beckoned him closer, but Darrius remained still. 'I thought not. It is strange that you come only once my father was murdered. He might have exiled you, but your exile did not end with his death. It was a kinder mercy than I would have given you.' Raiden plucked the crown from his head and tilted his head side to side. 'Have you ever worn a crown, Uncle? I suppose not. It's terribly heavy. Not just the burden of the entire kingdom, but it is made of gold, after all.' He sat back down on the throne, dropping the crown onto the cushion. 'You know, my father once told me that thrones are not made for comfort. That a king must endure discomfort for his people, so he may know their struggle.' Raiden swung a leg over the arm of the throne, lounging across it. 'He was right, it's as comfortable to sit on as a rock, but I can look past this. It is a price I would pay for my people. Would you like to try it, Uncle? Perhaps you can endure the discomfort better than I.'

Darrius shouldered the guards off of him and rose to his feet. 'Get off the throne, boy.'

'And who might make me do that?'

The sound of metal scraping against metal filled the room. Guards from around the hall had drawn their swords and were striding towards the throne; a handful of nobles had shirked their outer robes and drawn discreet weapons. More than a dozen guards rallied to Darrius' side, pushing past nobles as they retreated, not wishing to be caught between Darrius and the semi-circle of guards that stood between them and the king. Islo and five others stood, weapons drawn; two of Darrius' escort had blades to their throats, betrayed by the others in their company. Serana pulled at her son, tugging at his sleeve to leave, but Raiden ignored her, swung his legs back to the floor and leaned forward. 'What is this? A mutiny?' He rolled his eyes. 'So predictable.'

'You father was careless, and you follow in his footsteps. I say it once more. Get off the throne.'

'Now, why would I do that? You are outnumbered.' Two doors boomed open from either side of the throne, making Serana jump. Soldiers clad in black streamed into the hall, taking a place in protection of the king. Within the crowd of nobles, clothes were shed, black armour taking their place. Swords gleamed, and before Darrius and his guards could react, blades were pressed to their throats. The remainder of the palace guards that had not stepped to join either side lingered at the back of the hall, bewildered.

Raiden rose to his feet. 'Did you think I were so naïve as to not expect you had infiltrated my court? To not think that you walked among those closest to me?' His voice carried effortlessly, power and confidence reverberating from every word, and Serana realised she was no longer looking at her son. He was gone, lost to the jewels of a crown. She tried to speak, but he ignored her.

'You plotted an act of treason, and whilst I cannot prove you killed my father, I think this is enough proof that you sought to seize the crown. As the king of this land, I sentence your men to die.' With that, knives were ripped away from throats and swords thrust through ribcages. Blood-curdling groans filled the hall and Serana felt dizzy. Darrius paled, but was thrown to the base of the dais. Yells and shouts came from the remaining nobles, but none dared move. The council stood off to the side, uncharacteristically quiet.

'Allow me to introduce the Última Sombra—the Last Shadow. They are the last thing my enemies shall see, and even then, they shall never truly see them. I took the liberty of recruiting those most loyal to my father,' Raiden said, leaning back. 'Those who he had known and trained—the finest men of Corizon. They have all sworn their lives to me. What do you think, Uncle?'

Darrius trembled, surrounded by blood and black-clad soldiers. His eyes darted between them, then back to Raiden. Serana leaned forward to whisper in her son's ear. 'Remember what I have taught you. It is stronger to send a knife in the shadows than a sword in daylight. Serve the king's justice with the blade of another man.'

Raiden tutted. 'But where's the fun in that?' Holding a hand out, a squire hurried over and offered him the hilt of a sword. Raiden gripped it and drew the blade, admiring it before returning his gaze back to the hall. 'Red certainly adds quite the charm to the room, don't you think? Tell me, did you really think I would be as easy to kill as my drunkard father? You made a mistake sparing me that night, now you may learn the consequences of your own naivety.'

He scanned down the blade as he descended the stairs, looking at the lettering inscribed on the blade. 'You know, all great swords have names. It's a shame its first blood will be yours, but I suppose one cannot hope to slay worthy men with every swing.' Raiden stretched out his arm and let the tip of the sword rest on the bridge of Darrius' nose. The man trembled, staring up at the king. He moved the blade to his throat. 'What about *Silencer*?'

Raiden held himself for a moment, and Serana worried he would act. Instead, he retracted the sword and sat on a step higher up, out of reach. 'Alas, my mother has taught me well. Underestimate a man, and you won't get another chance to learn from it. Once I had assembled my father's finest men, I asked them to gather those who would swear fealty to me. I then demanded a list of names who were previously sworn to my father, but not named by my men. There is a difference between serving a king and serving the crown. Those who do not serve the crown lie behind you. Those who stand are the honourable men. I ask you now, Uncle, are you honourable?' He raised his eyes to the remaining nobles and council members, many staring mutely. 'Will you kneel in the blood of my enemies and swear fealty to your new king?'

A murmur of consent swept rustled from those who remained, but it was Darrius who spoke loudest. 'Of course, my king. I am yours to command.' The relief in his voice was clear, and Serana nearly spoke, ready to caution against such mercy. Raiden turned his back on the prisoner, just as Darrius was slipping his hand into his jacket, but he froze, his hand coming away empty.

'I wouldn't bother,' Raiden said, shaking his head. 'I turn my back and you reach to cut me down. Are you so desperate that you would sacrifice your own life?' Raiden faced the man, disgust on his lips. 'You would stab me in the back, just like you did your brother? I may be new to wearing the crown, but I know how this game is played.' He offered his hand to the soldier who had earlier forced Darrius to his knees. From within his cloak, he drew a long, straight dagger and handed it to the king. 'I'm surprised you didn't notice him take it. He's not the gentlest of creatures, though I'm sure you would agree he can throw a punch.' The soldier kept a plain face, but a hint of amusement sparkled in his eyes, as though the comment were the highest praise. 'Do you not think it would be ironic, Uncle? To kill you with your own weapon?' He held the blade to the light, then lifted a corner of his cloak and slashed through it, cleanly cutting through the fabric. 'Sharp,' he observed.

Fury flashed in the rebel leader's eyes. 'Do it. Do it, you swine. Enough games. Others will take my place, I swear it. You won't last on the throne.' He spat the words, revolted by the sight of the boy.

Raiden turned to his mother. 'Do you hear how he speaks to his king, Mother? I should cut his tongue.' Serana nodded, uncertain yet impressed. This was not the boy she had raised. Where this king had come from, she did not know, but a smile crept across her lips.

'You must make an example, Raiden. Ensure he is the last.'

'Indeed,' he said, as though deep in thought. 'Uncle, you request a power play, a demonstration of my capabilities, so here it is.' Raiden turned to the doors behind the throne. 'Bring them in.' At the command, the doors swung open and two Última Sombra marched forward, each dragging a woman. Both kicked and fought, but their captors gave no sign of struggle.

'No,' Darrius shouted, scrambling forwards, but a firm hand pulled him back and shoved him to his knees.

Raiden smiled and faced the women. 'Auntie, cousin, how quaint of you to join us. It has been some time since we shared one another's presence.' Neither replied. Despite their resistance, eyes were wide and their shaking hands blatant. The elder of the two had a dagger pressed between her shoulder blades, whilst Serana's niece was bundled forward, her hair lost in the knotted grip of a gauntleted hand..

Serana's heart faltered. She rushed to her son's side and pulled at his arm 'Raiden, no. You wish to make an example, not an enemy of a people. Do this, and there will be no forgiveness.'

Raiden shoved her off. 'You are wrong, Mother.' He turned and faced the gathering, eyes watching on. 'I wish to send a message,' he declared, 'to any who might oppose me. The crown does not rule with mercy, it rules with justice.'

'Leave them,' the strained voice came from below. 'They have no part in this.'

Raiden tutted. 'You asked for a demonstration, that I can do what must be done for the good of my people.' He turned to the girl but Serana stood between them.

'Enough. Know your battles, Raiden. Your quarrel is not with women and children.'

He narrowed his eyes. 'Perhaps not, but a blade will not teach him.' He pointed his sword to Darrius, who stared helplessly to his wife and child. Raiden's gaze flicked to the soldier holding the girl. The hulking man pulled his hand from her hair before planting a firm palm into her back, propelling her forward. She stumbled, her foot slipped, and she fell. The first few steps she screamed, then she was silent. Ice ran down Serana's back and she made to advance on her son, but another soldier, black armour shining, blocked her path, wrapped an arm around her waist, and lifted her to the side.

'Be gentle with her,' Raiden ordered, 'but keep her quiet. She must watch and learn how to properly rule a kingdom.'

At the bottom of the dais, Darrius dragged himself towards the limp body of his daughter. For a moment, the hall was quiet aside from that of a sobbing mother.

'Mariss,' Darrius said. 'Mariss, speak to me.'

Her shoulders trembled, and she lifted herself from the floor. Dripping from her now-crooked nose, blood stained her dress.

'You see, Uncle. She is just fine.'

'Bastard,' he roared. 'You leave my family alone.'

Raiden advanced on him, dagger in one hand, sword in the other. 'Like you did mine? You murdered your own *brother*. You filth. You rabid dog. I should kill you where you kneel and rid my kingdom of scum as foul as you.' Rage made the dagger waver, but Serana watched as he took a shaky breath. She pushed against the arm, but no matter how hard, it held like stone.

'Fortunately for you,' he said, 'your life will be spared. Perhaps I'm weak, but I am nothing if not just.' One of Última Sombra stepped forward and dragged Darrius by the collar before dropping him onto the steps. Raiden let his gaze sweep across those who watched. Every onlooker was silent, pale, unmoving. Many stood away from the others, as though not trusting the people they had arrived with or avoiding the blood of those they had.

Raiden returned to the throne, passing Darrius' dagger to a guard and resting his own sword at his feet. He smiled to his aunt as she glared at him, hatred pouring out of her. He took his seat and pressed his fingertips together, elbows resting on the arms. The guard handed the dagger to the Última Sombra that held the woman, replacing his own weapon with the traitor's blade.

'Here is my solution,' Raiden said matter-of-factly. 'You attacked my family, so I'll attack yours. You took someone dear to me, so allow me to do the same.' He spoke calmly, yet his voice seemed to travel, winding its way around the pillars and echoing back to him. 'It was once my father's belief that the king should wield the blade of justice, yet my mother has always taught to let blood be spilled by the hands of another. I am yet to decide my own opinion, but today my mother reigns right.' He looked to his aunt, and at the slight incline of his head, the Última Sombra grabbed her hair and yanked, pulling her head back and exposing her throat. The dagger was across her throat before she could shout, replaced instead by a sputtering gurgle. Serana grimaced, but she forced herself to look on.

Mariss cried out as the Última Sombra released her mother's body. It tumbled forward, bouncing limply down the steps, leaving a trail behind it until it slapped to stillness. Marris sobbed but remained still.

'And so it has ended,' Raiden growled.

A bang came from the end of the hall as one the doors shut. Some started, others searched for the source. Serana spotted a space where a palace guard had stood moments before, a handful of others stood, shifting uncomfortably, perhaps wishing it were they who had left. One of the Última Sombra stepped beside the throne. 'Do you wish for his head, my king?'

'No. Let him go. Rumours carry strength among the people. Let it be heard.' The soldier took a step back, resuming his position as the dagger was returned to Raiden. Darrius glared from the base of the steps, tears brimming.

'You never did have the stomach for this, Uncle. Here,' he tossed the dagger down the steps, letting it clatter to against the stone. 'Keep it. A reminder to think of the consequences of your actions.'

Darrius crumpled, as though the fight had finally left him. Mariss knelt by her mother's body, clutching her lifeless hand to her chest.

'It hurts, doesn't it, cousin? Do you feel your heart? The ache spreading with each beat. That's what your father did when he killed our king. Not just to me, but to all of his people. You agree that he had to be punished for causing such pain, don't you?' A muffled sob was her only reply. Raiden raised an eyebrow. 'Mariss, it is dangerous to ignore your king when he addresses you.'

A moment stretched out. 'Dammit, Mariss,' her father shouted, 'say something.'

She jolted and looked up, her chin red with drying blood. Her voice came as a strained whisper. 'Yes, my king.'

'Good,' Raiden purred. 'Then you will understand that I am not finished. He must pay for the pain he has inflicted upon the whole of Corazin.'

Serana shoved herself forward, breaking momentarily from the solider behind her. 'That is enough, Raiden. You have sent your message.' Thick arms crushed her chest and a hand clamped across her lips.

Mariss gasped as two guards lifted her by the arms. In a single, swift motion, one drew his blade and thrust it through the base of her skull. It burst through, splitting her lips as she choked on it. She was dumped beside her mother. A member of the crowd vomited, others shrieked and another fainted. Her body stiffened and blood coughed around steel. The blade slid out with a harsh, grating sound.

An inhuman noise came from Darrius as he scrambled for his daughter, but hands hauled him back, throwing him onto the steps. 'You monster,' he cried, pulling himself away from the sharp edges of the dais. 'She was a child.'

'She was a year older than I, and I can only wonder what you sought to do to me. Your daughter was no child.'

Raiden stood at the top of the steps, regarding the scene before him. Serana gave up fighting against the man who held her. Sticky puddles at the bottom of the dais reflected light from outside.

'Have I made myself clear?'

Darrius stared to his family, a crippled man. He nodded, eyes glazed.

'Then my personal message has been understood. You will take another message to my enemies, to those who follow you.' He gathered his sword, then stood before Darrius, holding himself to his full height. 'I took my mother's advice and let others kill for me, but that was a personal matter. A vendetta, if you like. My father believed only the king should serve the king's justice, and the crown is too heavy a burden for the people to bear. If I let you leave here the same man, you will only return. Allow me to dissuade you.' He stepped back and looked to Islo and the palace guard. 'Hold out his wrists.'

He struggled, but he was quickly overpowered. Darrius whimpered, cowering away from the boy. 'The king's justice is two-fold,' Raiden continued, addressing the audience. 'I will surrender to mercy, though if he were not blood, death would be the only punishment.' He slashed the sword through the air and two hands dropped to the floor. A long, carnal groan filled the air and Serana's skin crawled. She longed to charge forward, to snatch the blade from him and save what she could of the situation. Yet, she could feel the power she had once held over her son lift from her hands like petals in a hurricane.

A hate-filled stare came from withered eyes. The king smiled. 'Return to your rebels,' he commanded. 'Let us see who how many will follow a cripple.'

Raiden turned, climbed the dais, and rested his sword across the arms of the throne, the blade wet. He plucked the crown from the cushion, placed it on his head, letting it slip haphazardly down his head. He made for one of the doors behind the throne but paused. She felt herself tense under his gaze. 'Mother, I would walk with you.' He turned one last time and regarded the traitor hunched at the bottom of the steps. The stare followed him still and Raiden's lips twitched in disgust. 'Blind him.'

Serana was marched forward, herded after her son. The sound of screaming resistance chased them, but as they stepped through the door, the screams turned from an animal terror to a pain so pure it made Serana shudder.

Plucking the crown from his head, he held it at arm's length before dropping it into the arms of a page. 'See that it is taken to Master Russell. He knows what to do.' He paused and studied his mother, though what he searched for, she could not tell. 'I would dine with you tonight. Until then, do not disturb me.' He nodded to the Última Sombra behind her, instructing him likewise. Raiden made to walk away, but hesitated and turned on his heel. 'Oh, and try not to go running off again. The council seek to use me, and your insight on condensing their numbers would be appreciated.' He strode off, a trio of Última Sombra marching after him.

Serana felt unsteady as she watched him go, the corridor tilting around her. Her tongue felt heavy and she blinked hurriedly to steady herself. Her mind whirled, but she surrendered to acceptance. It was done. Fate's path had been laid, and there was no turning back. Perhaps she could still reach her son before he was lost to the monster under a crown, though she wondered if her words carried any significance anymore. He had acted without her, summoned her and those of the court to his performance, and she had been cast aside.

The king's first act was complete.

Chapter IV

She hurled a shoe at the wall, swearing. 'I'll have their heads. All of them. This is *their* fault.'

'Perhaps,' Laila said stiffly, 'but I made those shoes for you to wear, not to assault the walls with.'

'If the bloody council had just sat back and kept quiet, Raiden would still have half his sanity. Now he believes he is untouchable, and arrogance like that will not keep his head on his shoulders long.' Serana paced back and forth in front of her hearth. The sun had set, and an autumnal bluster had pushed its way along the plains, finding its way through cracks and into her chambers.

'Grief changes people,' her handmaid observed, 'or perhaps it was only a matter of time.' Laila was sat near the bed, clicking a pair of needles together as she entwined bundles of wool.

'No,' Serana snapped. 'If they had given me a year, a half-dozen months, perhaps, I could have taught him enough. He would not be like... *this*! Now he has the entire kingdom at his disposal and reining him in will be like taming a stallion with the scent of an in-season mare up his nose.' She threw herself into a nearby chair, feeling like a trapped fox. She had tried to leave, to seek something that might distract her thoughts and find some insight into what was happening beyond the walls of her rooms, but as soon as she had opened her door, a soldier, clad in black, barred her exit.

'Is there anything I can get you, Your Grace' He had a thick voice, monotone and emotionless.

She had tried to get passed. 'I am going to take a walk.'

'The king has ordered that the queen mother stay in her chambers until summoned.'

She had glowered at him, disgusted at the new title. 'I order you to move aside.'

A twinkle of amusement shone in his eyes, but his face remained placid. 'The king has ordered that the queen mother stay in her chambers,' he had repeated. 'However, she is welcome to entertain guests.'

Serana had clenched her fists, stepped back, and slammed the door in his face. Laila had raised an eyebrow. 'How regal of you.'

Serana had stood, seething at being denied the limited freedom. 'What is he doing that he does not want me to see?'

'I believe there are a great many things a teenage boy wouldn't want his mother to see, and now, as the most powerful man in the kingdom, he will do it all.'

'You are not helping.'

Serana had scowled at her, but Laila had only smiled. 'Was I supposed to be?'

Serana was left to stew in her rooms, prowling and fidgeting. She had tried her embroidery, she had tried to draw with a stick of charcoal, but her usual patience was gone. Not knowing what was happening in the rest of the royal chambers ate at her stomach and made her chest tight. She had resorted to planning for every eventuality she could think of, but it had not taken long before her father's words had risen to mind. *You cannot plan for what will come, for it is that which you do not plan for that will come to be.*

She had resorted to chewing at a braid of hair when conversation came from the other side of the door. Sitting up straight, she smoothed her clothes and turned to face the fire.

The door closed and Serana rolled her eyes. 'Do you ever knock?'

'Now why would I do that?' a rasping voice replied.

'So I can tell you to piss off without having to look at you.'

She heard the smile in his voice. It made her want to smash a vase over his head. 'But then Your Highness would never hear the wisdom I come to impart.'

'What a wondrous day that would be.' She turned on him.

A thin man stood before her, robes flowing over his arms. Grey eyes studied her, and when he moved, she half expected his bones to rattle. His movements were, however, quite the opposite. He moved as though a breeze, treading as lightly as a ghost. *If only he'd become one.* 'What do you want, Serril?'

'To impart wisdom,' he said simply.

'If that is what you choose to call it. Hurry, then. Spout your schemes so you may leave all the sooner.'

'I can see the king's actions this morning have rankled you somewhat, as it has I.' He spoke as though admitting a grave secret and paused as if waiting for some response. She let his words hang in the air to be knitted into the wool Laila clicked at. 'Word of his actions is already travelling fast among the city folk. He knows how to cause a stir, your son. I must say, his actions were… commendable.'

'You approve of his actions?' she said, aghast.

He chose his words with care. 'I agree with the sentiment. The execution could have had a little more… finesse. The rebels needed a message, and at first light, their message will be dragged back by a horse. The nurses are caring for him as best they can. He is… understandably distressed.'

He moved further into the room and eased himself into a seat by the fire, letting the flames warm the feeble bones beneath his papery skin. Serana circled him, keeping her distance as though he were a rabid dog. 'You acted too soon. The council will have war long before peace settles our land.'

'Perhaps,' he nodded. 'It was never our intention to invoke conflict. Alas, we serve the king and kingdom, as you ought. This morning was as our king wished. You could have been part of the decision, Your Grace, had you accepted our invitations. You could have sat in on our councils instead of sending others to do the deeds that should be orchestrated by the king and his closest advisors.'

'You think I would sit and deliberate trade deals or negotiate excuses to further raise the taxes of our people, all so you can continue to dress yourselves in lavish garments and sip at aged wines. I hold myself in higher esteem than that. It is the play of egotistic merchants, only interested in further weighing down their purses.'

He looked at her, amusement touching his lips. 'I don't see you wearing any rough spun wool, and I doubt that your wine is the same watered-down filth served in inns throughout the city.' Serril tilted his head back, seemingly content in this forced company. 'Besides, I do as I do for the benefit of our kingdom.'

'My part is played to more significance than you could ever know, Serril.'

'Of course, Queen Mother, whatever please you. As much as I enjoy our verbal sparring, I thought you would care to know how your son's first day as ruler goes.'

She held her tongue and settled on the cushioned chair opposite. *It is a game of give and take,* she reminded herself.

'After this morning's… ramifications, King Raiden has assumed his other roles rather well. He has dealt with the farmers to the east, sending reinforcements to the towns there. He has reassigned Islo as his Captain of Arms and listened to the council's advice rather well. It has been ordered that the walls be doubly manned, and all scouts be intercepted.'

Serana kept her face plain, though how she cried out inside. These were not the decisions of a young king, and she was troubled at the decision to move men away when forces awaited them on the plains. 'And the treasury? Has a Master of Coin been named?'

The corner of his mouth lifted. 'Who else? The king has other, more important responsibilities to be worrying about such trivial distractions.'

Her blood boiled. *As soon as Kerrick returns, an unexpected fall awaits you, Serril.* 'You think he is a puppet? He has a mind of his own. Enjoy your victory while it lasts.'

A sparkle flashed in his eye, and Serana resisted a shudder. He was holding something from her. 'One day, the time may come that our king learns to rule on his own. When that day comes, he will still have a council to advise him. But his mother? What need does a man have for his mother once he is grown?'

She clenched her jaw and spoke through gritted teeth. 'Thank you for your time, Serril. It has been a pleasure, as always. I would be alone now.'

He bowed his head. 'Of course, Queen Mother.'

That bloody title, she thought sourly. He slipped from the room as quietly as he had entered.

'That man gives me goose-skin,' Laila said once he was gone. She set her work aside before taking the old man's place opposite Serana.

Dread had sunk into her stomach and Serana felt ill. 'What are we to do, Laila? I can feel the fate of the kingdom slipping from my fingers.'

'Aye,' Laila nodded. 'But into whose hands does it fall next?'

Serana sighed. She felt tired, and she surprised herself in wishing that Dessius were here, though not for his solutions or company. No, he would have preferred she were as far from the situation as possible. *I suppose I would have wanted to be in the midst of it if I were not,* she thought glumly, though to let go of the reins suited her just fine at that moment.

'Come on, Queen Mother,' Laila teased. 'I don't care what that bag of bones says. You might not be the reigning monarch anymore, but I'm not letting you leave this room without looking like one.'

Chapter V

Serana entered the King's Hall in a flourish of silk. A scarlet gown trailed to her ankles, and stitches of gold and white embellished the delicate design of a ruby necklace hanging around her neck. Blazing fires roared in the hearths at either end of the hall. Portraits of past kings watched over a long table, candlesticks burning along its centre. Staring from the base of a painting, Raiden studied the portrait of his father. Serana stood beside him, and for a moment, they shared in the late king's presence.

'They got his nose wrong,' he said abruptly.

'Not at first. The initial painting was almost lifelike, yet your father raged at it, insisting it was changed.' She recalled how she had teased him about it and how he had only reacted in playful jest. No blows, no cutting words. 'It was before he resorted to drink, when he was a king worthy of the title. The people loved him once, you know?'

Raiden glanced at his mother from the corner of his eye. 'Was I born, then?'

'You were an infant, but your father's strongest source of pride. He promised me you would be the finest king this land had ever seen, that all would prosper beneath your reign.'

'Did you believe him?'

'I did.'

'And now?'

She hesitated and faced her son. 'I believe you can be what your father saw. That, and so much more.' She cupped his cheek gently, admiring the only child to survive birth. 'You have grown up too quickly, Raiden. Fate has been cruel to us.'

'No,' he said, averting his gaze. 'I have risen to the need of my people. I am ready.'

'Says who? The council?' Serana made her way to the table. Raiden pulled a chair back, but she stopped him. 'A king sits at the head of his table.'

His cheeks flushed, but he allowed his mother to seat him. She took the seat to his right-hand side.

'The council believe I am ready.'

'Be careful listening to the council. Their words may seem whole, but their intentions are rarely as pure as they seem.'

He sat back as servants streamed from the kitchen, steaming plates of meat and vegetables balanced on fingertips. 'And your words, Mother? What might I make of those?'

She studied him a moment, ignoring the servant that filled her cup. Raiden waited until they were alone. 'Rumours have reached my ears. They say you were in the rooms of the beast master.'

Serana felt her eyes narrow, but she retained her composure. 'Who told you this?'

'So it is true?' he said, pulling away.

'Yes, I visited the beast-master this morning. I spoke with him privately, just as we speak now.'

'The rumours say you were not there for speech alone, mother.'

'And you believe these rumours?'

He threw his arms into the air. 'I don't know what to believe. Why may no one speak to me straight. These riddles and unsaid words make my head spin.'

She smiled sympathetically. 'Welcome to court, my king.' She leaned forward. 'Let me make you a promise. I will never lie to you. I will be as transparent as a mountain stream, but understand this: there are times that water runs too swift, times that you would be better to turn away than to wade into their depths. Trust in this: if you need to know something, you will hear it when the time is right, not when you wish it. It may frustrate you, it may anger you, but I do it to protect you. Do you understand?'

He studied her a moment longer, before nodding, trusting in her the way only a child can trust in his mother. They ate in silence for a few minutes until he dabbed at his lips and sat back in his chair. 'I would like your thoughts, Mother.'

'All you need do is ask.'

'This morning. Was I wrong in what I did?'

Serana slowed, set her knife and fork to the plate. 'For a time, you impressed me. You did what was right and just.'

A dark look settled over his eyes. 'And then?'

'I think you know where I disapprove.'

'He murdered my father. Regicide cannot go unpunished.'

'And nor should it, but you were wrong in drawing innocents into the quarrel. Women and children have no place on a battlefield. Do you think it was your aunt or your cousin that sent the assassins? I doubt they even knew of the plot until it was long complete. They are not tools, nor pieces in a game. If anyone raises a hand to harm you, treat them as you would any man, but until then, you treat them with the respect they deserve. Men and women are equal, Raiden. It is your duty as a king to ensure that the innocent are not drawn into the whirlwind of conflict.'

Raiden's jaw set. 'I want him to hurt,' he said quietly. 'I want his every waking moment to be pained. I never want him to smile again.' His knuckles whitened as his fist clenched. 'I took everything that brought joy to his life and made sure he watched it bleed. A debt had to be settled.'

Serana watched him, and spoke slowly. 'I understand, but justice and your kingdom's welfare should not be tainted by personal feelings.'

He crumpled, resting his head against the back of the chair. 'Then I have failed already.'

She considered him a moment. 'You have taken your first step, and Fate is guiding you to where you must go, but it is how you get there that determines whether you are the honourable king your father saw. Guard your emotions and rule with your conscious. The heart is a fool's guide.' She reached across the table and took his hand. 'Never forget that I am here to guide you. To lead you to rule as your father once did, so you may become everything your father and I believed you can be.'

Raiden met her eyes. Hope filled them, and for a moment, for a fleeting second, she saw belief in him and wished she could share in it. They finished the rest of their meal with light conversation and wine, planning loosely for the days ahead: a formal coronation, dealing with the rebels peacefully, and reducing the council to those Raiden trusted most. 'A new Maxia must be sought, too,' she said.

Raiden narrowed his eyes. 'Magic is outlawed and will remain so. I will not have assassins and murderers running wild. Creatures who are more beast than man have no place in this world.'

'Which is why we need a Maxia to protect and advise against them. Few will come forth if called upon, and even fewer can be trusted.'

'What about Duna?' Raiden asked. 'Does the Maxia there have an apprentice?'

'Not one they would surrender. They are not as easy to come by, especially not loyal ones. But you might be right. We must reform alliances with the northern kingdoms. Perhaps Fate has some good fortune ahead of us.' She sipped at her wine. 'Yet, we must wait until spring sprouts from the snows. We cannot hope to send messengers into the O'Pasos and expect them to arrive until the coldest nights are behind us.'

He shifted uncomfortably in his chair. 'We would be without a Maxia until then?'

'Winter will shield us. The winds and snows protect us, for a time at least. We have until the ice melts to form negotiations. If it is a harsh winter, they will be feeble and desperate. We will have to time it well, but a deal can be brokered.' She spoke with confidence, but she could only trust in Fate that the winds would blow strong.

As the fire in the hearths burned lower, Serana rose. The day's events had made her weary, and the wine numbed her cheeks; she hoped she might sleep peacefully. 'Goodnight, my king. Tomorrow, the first sun rises on your reign. May it be long and prosperous.'

Raiden pursed his lips, though his thoughts were elsewhere. 'May Fate leave our path true and journey clear.'

She retired to her rooms, wondering at the contrast of the boy she had seen in the Jade Hall and the one she had dined with. *Perhaps he will rule well.* An Última Sombra was posted at her door, a different man from the one who had barred her passage earlier, and she nodded to him. Islo had already acted without her assent, but she decided she would let it pass. Some things were not worth arguing over.

Embers glowed in her fireplace and fresh linen dressed her bed. The floor was littered with lavender and water filled vases of flowers around her room. She exchanged her gown for her nightdress and Serana hoped that Laila had not waited long for her return. Had it been any other, they would have remained to see if she had any other duties to attend to, but Laila knew her well enough. It irked Serana that she needed someone to dress her, and Laila had designed a clever network of lace that meant she could undress on her own.

She often found that she sought evenings for herself. Her thoughts pressed to the forefront of her attention, and if someone else were present she would be unable to focus on either. Laila had not long been her handmaid, but she knew when she was wanted, and that was more she could have said for any other servant she had endured since her arrival at Corazin.

She climbed under the duvet, wrestling deeper into them. The air was cool, but a pan of coals slipped under the mattress made it all the more inviting. Once, she might have felt lonely in the large bed, but it had been many seasons since she had longed for her husband and she had grown accustomed to sprawling freely. She let out a content sigh. The day had not been as she had expected, but whilst she had feared for her son and his kingdom only hours ago, now she settled with a smile on her lips, believing that the future held more hope than she had dared admit in a long time.

Chapter VI

Sleep stole her swiftly, but it was not the sleep she had hoped for. She tossed and turned, imagination ablaze with images: Darrius standing on the throne, Raiden's head swinging from his fist; men clad in black, lying face down in pools of blood. The piercing scream of a man having his eyes put out filled her senses until they slowly evolved into the baying of hounds, first starting afar, but growing louder, nearer, until she could feel their breath on her neck.

She jolted awake, her heart racing as her thoughts tried to keep up. The room was dark, quiet. *A dream,* she told herself, lying back. *Just a dream.* She sighed and closed her eyes.

The snarling of a dog made her eyes snap open. Serana held her breath, listening. A bark echoed beyond her door, travelling from somewhere in the hallway. Her stomach clenched, but she took a breath and swung her legs over her bed, not bothering to find slippers to protect her feet from the tiles. She eased the door open and peered out. No guard stood at her door.

Stepping into the corridor, she looked up and down, unsure of which way to investigate. In both directions, torches fluttered, casting shadows that taunted her imagination. To her left, the door to the Great Hall was open ajar, but a particular figure to the right caught her eye. Obscured by shadows, it spilled from around the corner. Curiosity tugged her towards it, and she surrendered to it, if only to reassure her of her sanity. Despite its stillness, she moved silently, all the while wondering why a hound would be in the royal quarters. *Pah! You are letting your dreams run away with you,* she chastised herself. Yet, the closer she came, the more certain she was, until not even the shadows could deny the shape of a boot. Her step quickened, then came to a halt as she rounded the corner. An Última Sombra lay on his chest. Part of his skull was cracked open and blood pooled around his head.

Serana's heart faltered. A deep growling came from the end of the corridor, then a yell. Serana turned to see a great hound crouched, ready to pounce on the body of a boy.

'Raiden!' she shouted. A man charged towards them ahead of her, his steps uneven. She set off at a run but could only watch as the dog leaped forward. As it did, a sudden yelp came from the dog and its body jerked. It hit the floor and twitched.

Nightdresses swirling around her thighs, she was only moments behind the man who had been ahead of her. The frail man bent to help Raiden up, but he knocked the offered hand aside. Serana pushed past and dropped to her knees, realising with a loathing that it was Serril who had been ahead of her.

Light spilled over them from within the library. To reach there, she had past Raiden's own chambers—the library only a short amble away. Raiden scrambled away from the body of the great hound, the pale white hilt of a knife protruding from its ribcage, the blade buried deep.

'What happened?' Serana said breathlessly, pulling her son into an embrace.

He pushed her away, eyes searching down the corridor to the side, and when he turned back, fire blazed within him. 'Where were you?' he demanded. 'Where is my guard?' Blood streamed down his arms, skin torn and scraped beneath the tatters of his sleeves.

'Hush, Raiden,' Serana pleaded, taking his arm to inspect the wounds. 'We must take you to the nurses.'

He snatched his arm back, then spun as a door crashed open from the end of the hall. Captain Islo charged down the corridor, sword drawn. 'My king,' he cried, 'rebels are in the city, we must—' He hesitated as he saw two bodies.

'Where were you?' Raiden shouted. 'Your king is attacked and you don't even know until the danger is no more.'

Islo joined the group, eyes wide as he took in the scene. 'It's not safe, yet. The palace guard have intercepted rebels attempting to flee. There may still be more.'

Raiden shook his head. 'How has this happened? Where were the guards?'

'They were stationed on your door, Your Highness. As I advised.' The captain floundered, trying to count the bodies that he had stepped over.

A palace guard approached from the corridor that Serana had just come from. He paused before the group, addressed them appropriately, then reported to his captain. 'The men on the doors to the royal quarters were killed by knives and quarrels. It's the same at every entrance.' He glanced down the corridor to his left. 'I have only counted two of our own within the quarters, sir.'

'Where are the rest?' Islo demanded, fighting to save face in front of the king.

'Missing, sir. They are unaccounted for.'

The vein on his forehead bulged. 'I want those men hunted down. Not one of them lives. I want the head of every one of those rebels on a spike before morning. Every door into the palace and into the royal quarters is to be manned. No one moves without the guard knowing of it. Dismissed.'

Raiden shook his head. 'I should have your head for this, Islo. Your men abandoned their post.'

'Indeed,' said Serril, wrapping his arms around himself. 'I cannot believe it was a coincidence that the guard were missing the evening of an attack.'

Captain Islo took a step back, horrified. 'How dare you. It is my duty to protect the king.'

'And a marvellous job you're doing of it.'

Serana cut in between them. 'Let us speak in the library. Raiden must rest near some warmth before he catches illness.' The group nodded, though she thought more to be out of the chilled corridors and away from the bodies that littered them. Raiden lingered a moment by the door and Serana followed his gaze. 'What is it, my son?'

He paused a moment, trying to picture something in his mind. 'There were three of them, down there. Three men. Two men dressed in plain clothes, yet they fought one another, and a guard fought with one of them.'

'Raiden, you are tired and shocked. There are only two bodies there. They must have killed each other.'

'No,' he said firmly. 'The guard was killed first, then the two men fought. I-I thought I saw the last man running at me with the knife. I saw it hit the dog, but when I looked back, the corridor was empty.'

Serana hesitated, then guided him inside. 'Perhaps it was your guard's dying act that saved your life. You were in no state to be concentrating on their battle.'

Serril was already taking a seat by a large table; Raiden leaned against it. Islo paced nearby. 'Your Highness,' Serril's voice rasped, crackling with the wood in the fireplace. 'If what you say is true, then the knife-thrower was not ours. Perhaps his aim was not as true as he had hoped. Perhaps the blade was not meant for the hound.'

Serana turned on him. 'Do not speak of such things. The man saved the king's life.'

'And how many guards are trained to throw a knife?' he asked, raising an eyebrow to the captain.

Serana shook her head, disgusted. 'How dare you plant such thoughts.' She went to close the door but hesitated as she did. The captain was by her side in a moment, sword part-drawn. 'What is it? Are they back?'

'No…' she said quietly. She peered closer at the dog, not believing what she saw. 'Cazdor?'

'You know the beast?' Raiden said from inside.

'She is from the kennels.'

Serril scratched his chin. 'An attack from within, perhaps.'

She shot him a glare before stepping forward and crouching to lay a hand on the dog. 'How could this be?'

'My Queen,' Captain Islo said, leaning down and slipping a scrap of cloth from the dog's collar. 'It'd appear the dog was on the hunt.'

'The hunt for what?'

'Not what, Your Grace. Who. It's how the dogs are taught to hunt men. They chase a scent from clothing.'

Serana took the cloth from him and rubbed it between her fingers before stepping back into the library. Islo shut the door behind them while she set the scrap on the table.

Raiden leaned closer and shuddered. 'It's from my cloak. From this morning, in the Jade Hall.' His cheeks burned and knuckles whitened.

Serana placed her hand on his shoulder. 'Be calm. Rule with your mind, not your heart.'

He pushed her hand off, standing free of the table. 'This was a personal attack on the king,' he cried. 'On my *life*. I will not idle.' He turned to the others around the table. 'How is it Darrius attacks me whilst confined behind bars? Bring me his head. The beast-master's too.'

'Raiden,' Serana snapped. 'Think on your orders. It would send a stronger message to walk the city tomorrow as though you had slept peacefully than to send knives in the night.' She pushed away the thought of them searching for Kerrick, only to discover that he had left earlier that day. There would not even be a trial. 'Let us first examine what we can.' She turned to Serril. 'Why are you here? What excuse do you possess to be trespassing in the halls of the Royal Quarters?'

'My lady, you cannot possibly suggest I am behind such a plot?' Serril recoiled. 'I serve the king, as I have done for years before this.'

'Answer the question,' she growled.

He looked between them, then sighed. 'If you must know, I could not sleep. The thought of assassins and unsheathed blades roaming our halls has kept me from rest. So, I took to a walk, as I have every night since that grave evening. I find the night air has a clearing quality to it.'

Serana was ready to snap at him, but Islo spoke first. 'That does not explain how you came to be in the Royal Quarters.'

'Yes, yes. I was walking back from the palace gardens, when I saw one of your guards, Captain, lying across the floor, his throat cut and the doors to the quarters open, I hesitated not a moment. I raced in to ensure the wellbeing of my king, as any servant to the crown would. I went first to the king and told him to seek refuge in the library.' As he spoke, he looked to

Raiden, who nodded, confirming the tale. 'I then went to find the Queen Mother, to bring her to safety, too.'

'I did not hear you at my door,' she sneered.

Islo nodded. 'I heard the dog before I could reach you. I turned immediately, realising my mistake in leaving the king, but it was too late. When I had returned to the corridor, the beast was already upon our brave king. I tried to reach him as quickly as I could, and I am only glad that the knife reached you before I could—I doubt I could have turned the hound away.' He left his account to linger as they considered it.

'From what I witnessed, it seems true,' Raiden said grimly.

The captain then gave his own account, claiming that he had received reports that some of the guards had been murdered whilst on patrol. As soon as he had heard the news, he came to his king's protection. Again, the group nodded, unable to pick apart the alibi.

Serril frowned. 'My queen, how come you came to be here?'

'I will not justify such a poorly thought question with an answer. This is my son, and the Royal Quarters.'

'Ah, but was it not true that you visited the beast-master this morning? The kitchens were rife with the gossip. Surely you heard the hound before any of us?'

'This is preposterous,' she cried. 'Islo, you cannot fathom such accusations?'

He looked to his boots. 'My king,' he ventured. 'The man who escorted your mother from her trip this morning reported that she spoke of….'

'What?' Raiden's eyes flared, his voice a restrained growl. 'Tell me, now'

'Uncomely topics, Your Grace. Brothels.'

'You see,' Serril cried. 'She looks for another to warm her sheets, and not even a week since her husband has passed.'

'This is ludicrous,' Serana snapped, but she could see an idea gathering in Serril's eyes.

'It is as I told you, my king,' he said, ignoring Serana and speaking solely to her son. 'She lusts for power. I said she would undermine you, but I did not think she were capable of... this.'

Raiden spoke slowly, not taking his eyes off of her. 'Why were you with the beast-master this morning? In his private quarters.'

'Raiden, I told you I would give you the answers to questions when the time is right, not when you wish it. This is one of those—'

'Enough,' he snarled, startling her. 'I am the king, and I wish to hear it now.'

She glanced to Serril, amusement dappled on his lips. He raised an eyebrow, challenging her. A chill ran down her spine. 'Not here. A man's life is at risk.'

'You see,' Serril jumped in, shock and distain returned to his features. 'She plots against you, my king. She puts another's life before your own and seeks to take the crown from you. Had she been here this morning, I doubt she would have assented to your succession of your father, and who knows where she disappeared to—scheming with rebels and outlaws, I'll bet. Trust in your council, my king. Your leadership will guide Corazin to greatness. The city needs you. You must not allow those who block your path to prevail. Cut her down, Captain. The crown cannot fall to treason.'

Captain Islo did not move, but Serana took an involuntary step back. 'You cannot believe the words of a snake,' she said, but as she stared to Raiden, her heart sank.

The king spoke quietly, arms trembling, lips pulled tight. 'I cannot argue his case, Mother. There is too much you cannot defend, and I cannot ignore his wisdom.' Her eyes widened as he turned to Islo. 'Take her to the cells,' King Raiden ordered. 'Search the palace for any who do not belong and let them join her. Ascertain those who gave their lives tonight. I will inform their families personally tomorrow. The heads of those who have committed treason will stand at every gate on the inner wall. There will be no further attempts to usurp the crown. I *will* have peace.'

Captain Islo took hold of Serana, but the fight had left her. Her chest ached, and her legs felt unsteady. 'Raiden,' she whispered, 'do not do this. Do not make this mistake. Blades lie closer to you than you know.' Her eyes flicked to Serril. She knew he was behind it. She knew he was the orchestrator, but she knew not how.

Tears brimmed in Raiden's eyes, but he turned away, walking to a corner of the library. 'Take her away.'

Serril smiled as the captain of the guard marched her away. 'You played the game well, Queen Mother.

Admirably so.' She thought to shout, to curse him. Instead, she found her feet and walked in front of Islo, retaining what dignity remained. Outside, four Última Sombra guarded the doors. She hung her head, numb as they stepped through chambers. Guards formed a blockade in front of the doors to the Royal Quarters. Captain Islo paused to relay orders, though many were already tending to the dead. Despite this, he did not pass her to another, nor did he attempt to say anything to her. Serana could only watch as servants and visiting nobles were dragged from chambers and corridors, screams of fear and confusion echoing off of stone.

'It is a grave time indeed,' he said to no one, though his voice was burdened with sorrow. He walked her across the palace grounds and beyond its walls, into the cold belly of the dungeons. He let her walk herself, opening the cell door for her. 'I am sorry, Queen Serana. I know not who to trust, but I know that I serve the king. I must do what I think is right.'

She nodded, vacant. 'Then protect him. Watch that viper and the other members of the council, and let no harm befall him. Serve your king as I could not serve my son.'

He studied her a moment, then swung the iron door shut, letting it clang. Boots retreated up the steps, and another door slammed shut. Serana felt her way to the wall and slid to the floor, knees against her chest. She pressed her forehead to her knees, closed her eyes, and stole breaths of chilled air.

Morning was a long way away.

The Rogue

Chapter VII

The door boomed shut behind him. Raised eyebrows followed his exit as he tossed his helm aside and ran. 'Monster,' he muttered to himself. 'He's a monster.' Theon burst into the courtyard, heading for the barracks. *I'll be gone long before anyone comes looking.*

He kept his head bowed but continued on, not meeting the gaze of any he passed, especially not those wearing the coat of arms—those whom he served with. *Had served with,* he reminded himself. *I'm done.* He let his feet carry him over cobbled stone, planning as he slowed to a striding walk. *South. I'll go south and find my cousins in Oreth, or maybe Purth, start anew there. Find a wealthy merchant and offer my service.* A door interrupted his path and his thoughts; the barracks towered over him, two stories tall. He closed his eyes, stole a breath, and hoped no one was inside.

The mess room was empty. Over the fire, a thick broth bubbled in a cauldron; a wedge of cheese and loaves of bread sat plated on slabs of wood on the table. He passed them without a glance, stepping into the dorm and rushing to the chest at the foot of his bed. Theon threw the lid open and studied his belongings. There was not much, but more than he could comfortably carry. His eyes flicked to the bed. *They'll be more bothered by desertion than a missing sheet.* He threw the duvet off and untucked the corners before throwing his few belongings into the centre: several over-shirts, his breeches and a jerkin, and a few keep-sakes from his mother.

He was just tying the knot on his pack when he noticed his armour. Getting beyond the walls unrecognised would be nearly impossible. He stripped himself of it quickly, letting the heavy armour clatter to the floor. Reluctant to leave the leather jerkin, he exchanged his undershirt for another before shrugging back into the jerkin. He paused at his belt. *A palace guard's sword will be obvious but....* Tales of bandit gangs harassing travellers rose to mind, and he left it on.

Lastly, he wrapped his cloak around his shoulders and made sure it hid the hilt of his sword. The final item in the chest was a hunting knife. He paused, feeling the weight in his hand. Sam had given it to him when they had completed their training. 'A gift,' he had said. 'Should your sword fail you and the day comes that I'm not by your side.' They had laughed at the preposterousness of it.

Theon stared at it, guilt knotting his stomach. Sam had had it made for him: a bone handle with a long, curved blade the length of his hand. Theon sighed and slipped it into his waistband, tied the corners of the sheets together and weighed the bundle, nodding approvingly. Lastly, he slipped his bag of coin on top. Working in the ranks, the guards were paid perhaps not handsomely, but enough. Theon had saved every coin he could, choosing to let his colleagues spend theirs in the brothels without him; his presence at Corazin's taverns was far from common. He patted the smaller pouch of coin that hung on the inside of his trousers, secured to the waist.

He flipped the bottom of his shirt over the pommel of his sword, hauled the pack onto his shoulder, and made for the door into the mess room. Theon froze as the door to the barracks opened. A man with dulled golden hair looked back at him, his defined jawline set. Sam looked Theon up and down, frowning. 'What're you doing? Thought you were in the palace 'til shift change.'

'Could ask you the same thing,' he stalled, letting his arm drop and stepping in front of the bundle, attempting to conceal the white pack.

Sam raised an eyebrow, stepping inside. 'It's colder on the walls than I'd thought. Came to get cloaks for me and some of the others, but I'm on shift tonight—swapped with Hamish.' His eyes narrowed at the pack hanging behind Theon's leg. 'You know the serving girls will clean that for you? Islo give you the day off for finding the queen?'

'Queen Mother,' Theon corrected, finding a thrill at being able to share the news with someone. The gossip would find its way onto the walls and spread from there. All because of him. *No,* he told himself, *the fewer who know I was here, the better. At least until I'm far enough away.* 'I'm running an errand for her,' he recovered. 'Came to do the same as you.' He shrugged his shoulder, drawing attention to his cloak.

'Without your uniform? Islo will have you scrubbing boots for weeks if he catches you.' Sam tore a chunk of bread from a loaf. 'What sort of errand?'

Theon scrambled for an answer. 'She-she wanted a gown repaired.'

Sam rolled his eyes, talking around a mouthful of bread. 'You're a shit liar, Theon. The queen has her own seamstresses. Why would she want someone from the town to tend to her clothes? They're more likely to sell it than repair it.'

'It's true! There's a woman in the outer circle, best in Corazin, apparently.'

'Oh, old Traicy? I've heard the cook's apprentices talk of her.'

Theon tried to hide his relief. 'Yes, yes, that's her.'

He shrugged and stepped aside, leaning against the head of the table. 'Best you be on your way then— don't want to keep the queen waiting. Her shop's by the east gate, you know.'

'I've got the day to do it. Told me not to come back 'til it's done,' Theon said. He made to step past, but just as he did, Sam launched to his feet, dropping the bread and shoving Theon into the wall. Sam snatched the bundle out of his grip, and before Theon could right himself, the cold press of steel was against his throat. The white of a bone handle caught his eye.

'You're a shit liar. There's no Traicy. What's in the sack?'

'Mind your own,' Theon spat.

'Don't make me open it myself.'

Theon looked out of the corner of his eye, glancing between Sam and the bag. He knew he was safe from the blade—Sam would never hurt him beyond a training arena—but he knew if he moved to get the bundle, Sam would leap away and cut the contents free. Theon had never had much success against him in close combat. With sword or bow in hand, Theon would win even if on one leg, but as soon as they were close enough to trade blows, Theon's frame was too broad, and he had not the agility to keep up. Theon closed his eyes. 'Don't do this. You don't need to know.'

'Ah,' he grinned, 'but because you don't want me to know, I want to know even more. Where could you be going with this?' Theon he felt the pressure from the blade lighten, but he could not bring himself to look at Sam. 'Theon… that's your savings, and your clothes. Where are you going?'

Theon sighed. 'I'm leaving.'

'On a mission? For how long?'

'I'm not coming back.'

'What?' The blade disappeared. 'You're kidding.'

Theon shook his head and looked his friend in the eye. 'I can't stay here. I can't. You weren't there, Sam.'

He looked hurt and took a step back. 'Wouldn't understand what? You were just going to leave? Give up everything we've worked for?'

'You weren't there,' he hissed. 'Raiden's gone mad. He's murdering women and children, turning the Jade Hall red. I couldn't watch any longer, so I....'

Sam gave him a concerned look. 'Be careful what you say, Theon. Talk like that can see a man hanged.'

'I'd rather that than serve a monster.'

Sam watched him, as though waiting at any moment for him to give the game up and come clean. 'Are you well, Theon?'

Theon stepped towards him. 'Just give me back my things.'

'No,' he leapt back onto a bench. 'You're making a mistake and I'm not just going to let you leave. Not when you've given up everything else to be here, to wear this uniform.'

'Give up everything? I had nothing to give up. I wasn't the one to leave my estates and servants to follow some boyhood dream of protecting a city. It was the city that spat me out.'

'It was the city that gave you another chance,' he snapped. 'If it weren't for Islo, you'd be rotting in a cell, or worse, your head on a pike.' Theon glared at him but said nothing. 'Is this how you're going to repay them? By running away?'

Theon met his eyes. 'I swore to serve a king—an honourable man. I will not serve a monster who cuts the throats of women and throws their bodies down steps to rest at the feet of her husband and daughter.'

His eyes widened. 'What? This is madness, Theon.'

'The king's madness. The king is in the Jade Hall as we speak. He's already had his aunt killed, and I don't want to think what he's going to do to his cousin. Darrius is in there. The crown has sickened the king. He's blind with revenge and I cannot serve a man who does not think, never mind one who murders innocents.' A realisation came to Theon and he took another step towards him. 'Come with me, Sam. Flee whilst you can.'

'Theon,' he said in horror. 'I swore an *oath*, as did you. To serve the crown and whoever wore it. To break that? I can't.'

Theon nodded, but felt the disappointment in his chest. 'And I won't force you, but let me make my own decision. You know it's not one I take lightly.'

Sam watched him for a moment, then dropped the bundle to the floor. 'This's your decision? You know you can't come back? You're lucky I don't drag you to Islo right now.'

Theon nodded, before scooping up his bundle. He hesitated and looked towards the hunting knife.

'Oh, no. I gave this to a man I thought I knew. A man with honour, whose word was as strong as his back. It belongs in the hand of a man who would die for what he believed in, not one who flees like a kitten.'

They held each other's gaze for a moment. Theon longed to stay, to take the blade back and take whatever punishment would befall him. Sam would help him. He would get through it. Theon looked away. 'I can't serve the crown if I won't die for the man who wears it. I can't ignore my heart. Corazin will burn under his reign, and I will not be part of it.'

Sam's lips curled back in disgust. 'Then go,' he snarled. 'Get out, before I use this knife for what it was made for.' Theon turned to the door, but as he stepped through, Sam's words halted him. 'Theon, this city made you. Don't forget that.'

'I made my own Fate. This city turned its back on me, and now it's my turn to turn my back on it. Goodbye, brother.'

He pulled the door shut, but he still heard the words that slammed against the wood. 'You're no brother of mine.'

Theon hurried towards the inner wall, avoiding the southern gates. If they were looking, that is where they would expect him to go. Instead, he made his way east. He knew he should run, flee as quickly as he could, but he had to make a last stop.

One final visit.

Chapter VIII

The *Three Cascos* was quiet. A sign wafted in the wind, the image of three helmets stacked into a pyramid on it. Theon stepped inside. Smells drifted from the inn's kitchens and he yearned to collapse in front the fire and drown himself in ale and the chatter of strangers. Instead, he stepped up to the bar, addressing the inn keeper who was examining a glass before returning to scrubbing at the rim with a cloth. 'Excuse me,' Theon said, waiting to draw the man from his task. For a moment, the innkeeper seemed not to notice, working the cloth vigorously at the cup before holding it up to the window. Theon cleared his throat and the innkeeper set the glass down with a sigh. 'All our rooms are taken, lad. I have some of last night's meats and some bread, if food's what you're after.'

'Neither. I'm looking for someone. A maid who works here.'

The innkeeper gave him a knowing smile. 'They say a pretty word to get a penny out of you, lad. They promise every customer who comes through that door that they'll see them another evening. Let me save you time and face. None of my staff will leave with you. You cannot promise them more than they already have: a roof, food, safety. Do yourself a favour. Find women with softer hearts, and failing that, you'll find the brothels to be kinder than the girls here.'

Theon tutted. 'I'm not asking anyone to leave with me. I wish to leave something with one of your serving girl. Will you tell her I'm here?'

He looked Theon up and down, seemingly less sure of him. 'They're busy, lad, and I won't have any of them caught up in whatever shady business it is you're running. They don't have time for idle chatter with louts from the night before.'

Theon held his tongue and slipped his hand into his bundle before dropping the pouch of coin onto the counter with a thud. The innkeeper's eyes widened. 'Give this to Dhalia,' he instructed. 'She deserves to be free of this cistern. She wants to move to the villages on the outskirts and open a shop of her own. This'll help.'

The innkeeper licked his lips and glanced at him. 'Aye, that it should.' He set the cloth down but wrung his hands regardless. 'What's she done to earn a king's ransom?'

'Killed a king,' Theon said, rolling his eyes irritably. 'I have not asked her to leave with me because she deserves a man who can care for her and cherish her. I cannot give her my heart when I know she would be happier with another's, so I give her this.'

The innkeeper eyed him. 'You have a lot of faith in strangers, lad. Few would trust the coin to reach her hands.'

'You're a man of your word, and I'll have yours from you. You look after those who deserve it. I've seen you throw out men twice your size who have caused trouble when they had plenty more coin to spend, and you've given hot meals to those who cannot afford it. If you wanted this coin, you'd have taken it already.'

He winced slightly. 'You say you're not here to take a girl away with you, but with this, she surely won't stay.' He weighed the pouch on his palm. 'Who should I say has given this girl her dreams?'

Theon hesitated. In truth, he wasn't sure she knew his name. She had always been kind to him, smiled to him and sat down with him when she was supposed to be working. She listened to his stories and laughed at his misadventures. She often served him ahead of those who had been waiting before him, and his plates had always seemed to contain extra portions compared to those on other tables, but his name had never been mentioned. He reasoned that she might do this for any to get an extra coin, but there were things she did only with him. She called him her knight, though he had insisted that he was not one, and he knew of no others that had heard of her speak to her lessons with her father, that her delicate hands could craft something elegant from a lump of clay, and her father had always complemented her skills with a paintbrush. She had even once shown him one her father made, and she had decorated with fields and summer flora.

Theon smiled. 'Tell her that an admirer of her craft wishes that she pursues what she loves, and that he wishes her happiness.' He hesitated a moment, then added, 'And tell her goodbye.'

The innkeeper smiled sympathetically. 'Aye, lad. I'll do just that.'

Theon thanked him and left the warmth of the inn. The air outside had a chill to it. Summer had long passed and winter would be upon the city within a few weeks. Theon lifted the hood of his cape and strode towards the eastern gates. Around him, people bustled and went about their business. It had often irritated him when people stepped in his way, and when he was wearing his uniform, there had always been a clear path ahead. Now, as a woman dawdled in front, he found himself calm. It was as though the city wanted him to experience it again. So he turned his attention away from the people, and for the first time since he had passed his training, he looked at the buildings and the wares within.

As a boy, he had always stared at the merchandise. He had scurried about the streets and entertained himself with whatever caught his attention. Once he had completed his training for the palace guard, his focus had shifted. At all times he had watched the people, keeping an eye out for pickpockets and thieves, for any sign of those who might cause discontent. It had tainted his view of the city, only paying attention to those worthy of a peace-keeper's attention. He had forgotten to look at the city that had raised him, forgotten the hiding places and short-cuts he had known as a boy, seeing it less as a place of adventure and more as a place of threat—something he had never seen until trained to see it.

He approached the gates and forced himself to relax. He loosed the breath he had been holding and tried to look disinterested. No one stopped him or called out to question him. After all, why would they question a man leaving the city? As far as the guard were concerned, someone leaving the city was one less person to worry about. When the walls were to his back and open land lay ahead of him, he let the grin free. He turned and looked back, wondering if he would ever return; he realised he would be quite happy if he never did.

Wind rolled across the plains. Theon shivered with the grasslands as he tightened his cloak around him, cursing himself for not replacing his woollen shirt sooner. It was only shortly after midday, and the sun was high above. He thought that the day might have been pleasant had the breeze not snatched away any warmth the second it touched his skin.

Despite the cold, Theon was in high spirits. The air had helped to clear his mind, and with each step that he took, the surer he was of his decision. A sense of adventure tickled at the base of his ribs and he could not keep the smile from his face. *And why should I?* he thought. *My life is my own again. Fate has chosen a new path for me.* Occasionally, he turned and looked back to Corazin, but each time the city had shrunk more and more, becoming less grand: a molehill in the foothills of the mountain. *I've spent my whole life inside those walls, stuck in their shadow and sworn to die for those there with me, but how many would have done the same for me?* The thought of Sam rose to mind, but he pushed it away. He had been right: there was no going back now.

Every night of his life had been spent inside those walls. He might have ridden the lowlands around the city, scouting and hunting, even trained in the Pasos, but he had never left. He felt giddy at the thought of freedom, of doing something so many had spoken to him of, many of them hoping that Fate had success and prosperity waiting for them in Corazin. Now, here he was, at the beginning his own journey, hoping for the same in another land.

Ahead, the road stretched on until the village interrupted it in the distance. Rebels were camped to the south and east of the squat village, thin trails of smoke rising from campfires. Theon eyed them uneasily. If these were the men who had murdered the king, they were men Theon had no wish to encounter. He shuddered at the thought of Maxia prowling the camp. He wondered if they knew who he was, what he was doing heading south. He dismissed it. *Maxia may be powerful, but they cannot read minds. That, surely, is a fantasy from minstrels' tales.*

Aside from farmers and local travellers, few shared the road with him, and as winter drew nearer, it would only become more so. Occasionally a trader passed—a straggler, trusting that Corazin would be their refuge, with most others already having chosen their winter roosts. He wondered how long it would be before he had somewhere that he could call his own.

The closer he came to the village, the more anxious he became. His palms began to sweat, and his heart was working faster than it should have been. The thought of Maxia preyed on his mind, and even just knowing they were near was making him want to run until the village was little more than a dot on the horizon.

At last, he relented and turned off the road, giving the village a wide berth. Tall grass brushed against his shins, birds swooped and dived, darting this way and that to catch insects he could not even see. As he walked, Theon eyed the village, wondering what life must be like growing up there, wondering what they thought of the city they supplied. *Yet, without the city, they could not be, either.* The surrounding villages and towns all supplied the city, but the reliance was mutual, if not equal. The harvests and animals fed the city, but without the skilled smiths, seamstresses, and carpenters that the city held, the villages would struggle to sustain, if at all.

The longer he walked, the more he truly began to fathom the threat that sat before the city. The rebel camp was larger than he had imagined, stretching farther to the south and spilling more round to the east, amassing for a distance behind the road. The sight made his stomach twist, and he suppressed the urge to run back to the city and warn of the scale of the rebels. There were at least a thousand and a half, but Theon could have been convinced of more. From the city walls, the village and encampment were visible, but at such a distance, and from such a height, little seemed threatening. Now, as he walked by, their sheer volume was worth his worry. He gathered his resolve and his cape and marched on.

The village was nearer to his back when the riders broke from the encampment. Theon did not see them until they had covered half the distance. Panic fluttered in Theon's chest, and his first instinct was to run, but never had he met a man who could out-run a horse. Besides, run where? The plains were vast and open; no shelter lay between him and the next town aside from a copse of trees in the distance. Instead, he tightened his hood around him, loosened his sword in his belt, and continued as though he had not seen them, hoping they might be galloping elsewhere.

'Ho there, traveller,' a voice shouted as the pounding of hooves slowed. Theon looked up but kept his hood around him. 'You look lost, traveller. What's your name?'

Two horses pulled rein either side him, shifting around him on opposite sides. Astride them, a young man—younger than Theon—watched carefully, one hand on the hilt of his sword; the other was older, with a tangled brown beard and thick eyebrows. It was he who had spoken.

'Perryn, sir.' Theon said, not looking him in the eye.

'Sir, eh? Hear that Warren? I'm a knight, a *noble*.'

The boy grinned but said not a word.

'Where are you travelling from, Perryn?'

'Corazin,' Theon nodded towards the city, cursing his politeness.

'And where'd you be going? Can't be far with a bundle that small.'

'I have what I need to get by.'

The man looked him up and down, pausing at the sword that hung from his hip. 'Aye, I don't doubt that, friend. You're a long way from the road. Another man might guess that you're avoiding it.'

'You wouldn't be wrong.' Theon spoke slowly, but his mind raced to fabricate his new personality. 'I don't much like crowds, you see. Seen too much of that in the city. Was after some peace for a bit. Besides, I was told to avoid the village. Reports were that a traveller might be harried for simply walking through. Said nothing about walking around it.'

The man's eyes narrowed. 'Where'd you say you were going, Perryn?'

'South.'

'So close to winter? Many would warrant it a fool's errand.'

He shrugged, trying to work some calm into his demeanour. 'Then perhaps I'm a fool,' he said, stepping away as the horse danced nearer. 'There was no work in the city, and a man has to do what he can to survive.'

A dangerous smile touched the rider's lips. 'And what's it you do for work, friend?'

Before Theon could reply, movement behind him lifted his shirt, revealing the hilt of his sword. Theon spun, drawing the sword and pointing it to the horse as it nickered aside, carrying the young man away. Theon kept a man at either arm, not letting them circle to his back.

'What'd you make of that, Warren?'

The boy's eyes narrowed, his own sword now drawn. 'Palace guard if I ever seen it.'

'Right you are, boy.' They stepped around him, swords gripped firmly. 'So, Perryn, what say you now?'

'A man does what we can to survive,' he repeated through gritted teeth. 'I wish you no harm, just let me pass.'

'No harm?' the bearded man said, eyeing the blade that pointed at Warren. 'This looks quite the opposite.' He shrugged and slid from his saddle, passing the reins on to Warren. The man seemed unbothered by the drawn sword, his own swinging from a limp wrist. 'Normally I wouldn't have even heard your name, but we've been watching you. Watched you all the way from the city, and something just didn't add up. Then you left the road, and,' he smiled, 'well, here we are. You're lucky. We might have use of you yet.'

'Jerrah?' the boy said uncertainly.

'Hush, boy. Don't interfere.' He flicked his wrist, sword spinning through the air in a flourish before dropping into a stance. 'Let's see if his lies add up.' His eyes narrowed, 'Or is he a thief as well as a liar?'

Theon swallowed and took a step back. Behind his opponent, figures raced from the camp towards them. His gaze jumped to the man as he leaped forward, slicing low towards Theon's ribcage. He threw his sword up, barely deflecting the blow as he staggered backwards. The power in the man's movements had

97

surprised him and he commanded an alarming amount of strength from his slimmer build.

Without slowing, Jerrah used the momentum from the deflection to let his skewed blade run to the side, using it to spin and change to a high, backhanded swing directed at Theon's shoulder. Again, Theon brought his blade up in time, but the power was too much, the edge grazing his shoulder.

'Good, good,' Jerrah purred, looking him up and down. 'Not just a sword for hire. Trained. Good reflexes.' He leaped again, crossing a startling amount of ground as he did. He thrust the sword for Theon's stomach, and had he not stepped aside, nicking the blade with his own, it would have pierced him. 'A clever fighter, too. Using your opponent's momentum against him.' Jerrah grinned as he circled him. Theon dropped his bundle, adopted a stronger stance. *He's toying with me. If he wanted me dead, my blood would already be soaking the grass.*

'What about your speed, Perryn?' He made to cut him again, feigning one way, then pivoting, attacking Theon's undefended left flank. Theon stepped quickly, treading down grass. Metal clashed, the clang stolen by the wind. Jerrah advanced further, not sparing him a second to recover. Blow after blow, Theon raised his blade, letting him skip forward in great strides. He watched his movements, searching for some weakness or old injury, any opening. None appeared. Every step was calculated, plotted two moves in advance. He seemed to know how Theon would block and already be moving into his next stance before Theon could recover.

A flurry of attacks went deflected, but not cleanly. One struck his ribs, snatching his breath away; another cut at his thigh, tearing his trousers and skin.

With each contact, Theon felt his anger grow, until, just as Jerrah retreated to make another observational comment, Theon snarled, charging forward. Jerrah blocked the counter but was unprepared for the body that slammed into him. He was propelled over the grass, sent rolling before springing to his feet.

'Good, Perryn. Very good,' he grinned. 'They train their guard better than most other cities.' Jerrah's advances became relentless, not letting Theon pause. Sweat matted his hair, and he found himself searching for a mortal blow, one that might risk his own health, but, if successful, the fight would be over.

An opening appeared where Jerrah had left his shoulder exposed. *He's tiring,* Theon realised with a grim satisfaction. He threw himself forward, swinging horizontally with all his might towards Jerrah's neck. The older man had two options: attempt a block and trust that he could defend the force of the impact, or strike first, spearing Theon's chest. If he did, he would have to hope that Theon's momentum would not carry the blade into his own flesh regardless. Either way, the fight was over.

Jerrah chose a third option. He moved faster than Theon had seen any man. Ducking under the blade, he side-stepped behind Theon, bringing the pommel of his sword down on the back of his knee. Theon buckled, and a powerful hand shoved his head forward, sending him sprawling face first into the grass. His sword spilled from his grip and before he could catch himself, the cool tip of metal pricked the base of his neck. 'Careless. You mistake a bluff for an error, and thus you pay for it. I'm sure even young Warren saw that attack coming.' The metal disappeared and when Theon looked up, Jerrah was collecting his sword from the grass. 'Yet, a good warrior,' he concluded.

The pounding of hooves registered in Theon's ears and the vibrations under his finger. He picked himself up, panting.

'Why does he live, Jerrah?' a voice demanded, muted on the wind. 'I won't have my men attacked and let the man walk away.'

Jerrah addressed the lead rider, scarcely out of breath. 'A palace guard, Mathias. From Corazin.'

'Far from the palace,' the man observed, studying the blade Jerrah offered him. He had thick black hair tied back into a tail.

'He could have information we need.'

The man nodded, watching Theon carefully. 'Take him back to the Maxia. Let her discover what she will. Perhaps then we might decide whether he's of use.'

'No,' Theon's heart stopped, and he took a step back. 'Please. Not a Maxia. I'll do whatever you want, just don't take me to a Maxia.'

Mathias raised an eyebrow. 'That's not for you to decide.' He turned his horse and sped off. As he did, Theon turned and ran. He got several paces before a weight crashed into the back of his legs. Hands grabbed him and trussed his arms behind him, but Theon kicked and struggled, catching one of the rebels in the ribs, earning him a grunt and a fist to the stomach.

Jerrah lingered a moment, then rolled his eyes as he stood before the men who held Theon. 'Unless you want him fighting you all the way back to the camp, you might want to try a well-placed blow.'

Before Theon could understand what he meant, the pommel of Jerrah's sword struck the side of his head and the plains sparked to darkness.

Chapter IX

He came around slowly, blinking until the room was clear. Without moving his head, he took in his surroundings. The roof sloped down sharply next to him and reached a peak not far above. It was dark, hazy. 'How long have I been out?' he muttered to himself.

Theon jolted as recollection came through him, but the pain behind his eyes kept him down. He was lying on a cot, and what he thought had been a room was a black tent. Candles burned, throwing smoke and foreign scents into the air. There was a desk opposite the cot, a chest next to it. At the desk, a figure sat hunched over a piece of parchment.

'Not long, thankfully,' the figure said. 'I was worried I was going to have to fetch a pail of water to wake you. The fools don't think beyond the moment at hand. I must apologise for their behaviour—Darrius would be disappointed to discover that we have turned to treating guests with violence.'

Theon shrank back against the wall of the tent. 'Are-are you the Maxia?'

The figure stood and turned to face him, curious amusement on her face. The woman had long black hair braided over one shoulder, her skin a darker complexion than was common in the north. She offered him a goblet. Theon eyed it warily. 'Wine,' she said. 'It'll help with the head pains. As to your question, yes, I am a Maxia, but you may call me Alyce.'

Theon narrowed his eyes, wincing as he sat up. 'Why am I here? Why didn't they let me go, or...' he trailed off.

'Kill you? Because you might be able to help them.'

He sniffed at the wine, taking a cautious sip as she watched. 'Help *them*?'

'I don't take sides,' she said, turning her chair to face him. 'My abilities are offered to those whom I deem it worthy. I am sworn to nobody, nor am I anybody's tool. I serve the land and the people who live on it, not the few who sit and take from them.'

'But Darrius wants to take the throne. He wants to govern Corazin with a council. You agree with that?'

Alyce nodded, pulling her chair to sit in front of him. 'He wants to give the power to the people, to let them decide their own Fate. Once the crown has fallen, I will leave the people to Fate, allowing them rule the land as they see fit—it is theirs after all.'

Theon frowned. 'But the people will never be able to make the decisions a king does. How could they be expected to know where to distribute troops, or grain, or cloth? It's too much responsibility.'

'It is too much responsibility for one man. If the people rule, the resources will go where they are needed, not to he who is most favoured. It will work because the people will make it work. We are selfish creatures: we get what we need to survive, and if we don't have it, we are rarely quiet until it is otherwise. Yes, there will be a time of struggle, but it'll right itself. I have seen it happen.'

Theon bit his lip in thought. 'What's this got to do with me?'

'Jerrah seems to think you were once a palace guard. This is correct?'

Theon nodded slowly.

'There is a plot to attack the city tonight. Fate has laid its path up to this point, but they search for as many routes that might lead it to the destination they seek. Darrius is at the palace as we speak.'

'His wife has been murdered,' Theon said gravely.

'His daughter, too,' she nodded. Theon looked up, startled, but she continued as though she had not noticed. 'He will not return the man he was, but he has served his purpose. There is no changing Fate's path once it is laid. The people have amassed, the plans have been made. We stand at the precipice of change. Now all we may do is walk the path that appears before us. The only choice we have is whether we drag our heels and stare at the ground until darkness catches us, or walk with a bound in our step and our chins held high.'

He watched her carefully as she leaned back. Smoke swirled around her; it was making his eyes sting. 'If you know this, then you know I can't go back.'

'It is why you must go back, deserter. You have two choices: return to the palace, aid the rebels and walk free, or refuse, and Jerrah will serve you a swift death. I wish it were not so, but freedom is what they fight for, and opposing them means you fight for chains.'

'That's hardly freedom,' Theon scoffed.

'Is it not? You have the freedom to choose. At least they are merciful, deserter. There are worse things in life than its end. Will you walk the path before you, or kneel and accept the darkness?'

Theon scowled. 'What do you need me for, then? If you can assassinate the king with magic, can't you do it again?'

Her eyes darkened. 'That was not I. Those were dark and twisted men, using magic against its natural purpose. Magic is found where there is life,' she said sombrely. 'Whilst death is a part of life, magic should only be used to nurture it. There are those who believe that Fate and magic are separate, that magic can guide Fate's path. I do not wish to test this, nor do I believe any man should be able to carry such power.'

Theon's eyes darkened. 'They were assassins.'

'Murder is murder,' Alyce shrugged. 'It matters not who dies, nor who pays for it. The loss of life is a tragedy all the same. Magic is not a weapon—not something with a single purpose. It's more like a hammer: you can use it to create something beautiful, or you can use it to cave someone's head in. The use is not decided by the tool but by the one who holds it.' She shook her head sadly. 'To use it as they do poisons their very beings.'

Theon closed his eyes and shook his head. *This woman makes no sense.* 'Enough. What is my role in this? And speak plainly, my head still hurts too much to pick apart your words.'

'Do you accept to help the rebels?'

'Do I have a choice?'

'There is always a choice, deserter,' she said kindly. He sighed, and she took his assent. 'Finish the wine. It'll help.'

He flinched away from her as she stood. 'What are you going to do to me?'

She turned and rummaged in the chest for a moment, before pulling out a pale, white piece of wood carved into the shape of a ram. A length of string ran through a loop in it. 'Darrius is a paranoid man. Rightly so, I suppose. Every man and woman in this camp has been verified against his or her word. If you have lied, I will know. If you intend to deceive, I will know. I'm afraid there will be no secrets between us, deserter. Do you wish to continue?'

Theon did not say anything. She held the necklace out to him. 'What is it?' he asked.

'An enchanted piece of wood carved from the Kaminjo tree. Not everyone is strong enough to withstand magic within them, nor can they control it. This ram will prevent you from becoming overwhelmed.'

'It's heavy,' he noted, weighing it in his palm. Looking closer, he observed a stain along its edges. 'And there's blood on it.'

'Try not to squeeze too hard.'

He looked up at her, unsure. 'You'll be giving me magic?'

'Not quite. I will channel magic into you to create a temporary bond between us. This will connect my mind to yours. From there, I shall begin my investigation.' She picked up a parcel from her desk and unwrapped a pale biscuit. 'It will help your strength return afterwards,' she explained. 'Don't fight it, you'll only make things difficult. The wine will have already helped to relax you, but you mustn't resist me, okay?'

Theon sighed, calming the nervous tremble in his fingers.

'Hold your hand out.' Alyce leaned forward, taking a breath. 'Focus on something. I will be quick.' He watched over her shoulder as a wisp of smoke curled up from a candle on her desk.

Her hand touched his, and fire shot up his veins. His back spasmed, and panic flooded through him. He could not move, and his body no longer listened to his mind. His vision swam, and the wooden ram burned in his palm.

A presence forced itself into his mind, sweeping away any thoughts. It surrounded him, and its vastness pressed against him. Theon's only reaction was to recoil, to hide within himself until it passed.

A sharp pain flared from his shin, and in that moment, the presence overwhelmed him. 'Relax,

Theon,' the voice commanded. 'Don't fight. Embrace me as I have you, then we will be done sooner.'

How do I do that? he thought, struggling to get his thoughts under control.

'Reach out, Theon. Relax.' He could hear her voice, but it was distant, in a place beyond where he had hidden himself.

How did she reply? I didn't—

'Theon, I'm with you in your thoughts, but you *must* join with mine, if not, the bond cannot be made. Make hast!'

Theon focussed himself, and instead of recoiling from the presence, he reached out towards it. The contact sent surging heat through him, and he instinctively retreated.

'Do not shy from it. Embrace it. You'll be safe, you have my word.'

Theon collected himself, and this time, instead of reaching out slowly, he flung himself into the energy that coursed around him, as though leaping from a riverbank to be swept away.

'Easy,' Alyce's voice grunted, yet he barely heard her. Instead, he felt the discomfort he had inflicted upon her, the side of the chair digging into her thigh, the weight of her hair over her shoulder, the readiness of her shoe to kick him again. He felt her relax.

Good, she thought, and he heard, but there was more. He could sense her relief and her approval. *Maintain this, and it'll soon be over.*

Her voice disappeared, yet he knew her intentions, just as she knew his. The voice within her mind was different to her spoken voice, yet he knew it belonged to her. Somehow, it was distinctly her own.

What was your childhood like? she asked.

He wondered what to tell her. He thought of life with his mother, the room in the roof that he grew up in, how he had survived on his own since he was a boy. *Good,* she said, and she sensed his shock. *I am in your mind, Theon. You cannot hide things from me. Who were your parents?* Again, without any conscious effort, he envisaged his mother, her bright eyes and kind smile, her patience. The image was tainted by his later memories, the ones of her lying in bed, eyes sunken and skin pale. He pushed the image away.

What are you most ashamed of? Alyce continued, the images seemingly nothing of consequence to her.

Theon remembered the time after his mother had died. He had been thrown onto the streets. That first day, he had not known what to do with himself, but as the nights passed, the reality of his situation weighed on him heavier and heavier. He remembered stealing a loaf of bread from a woman. He had not been small for his age, and he had always thought he must have looked rabid. He had cornered her, threatened her, and taken her purchase and her purse. It was a memory he had repressed, one from another life, but Alyce saw it and studied it.

You did what you had to do, she assured him, but he was still uncomfortable that she knew of it.

What are you most proud of?

He saw his training and sparring with Sam. Their first encounter had been practising with swords. The fight had been short. Theon had always fought effectively, whilst Sam had been previously trained by a swordsman. He moved from stance to stance while Theon fought with little regard for his own safety. After one deflection, Sam had turned with a flourish, and as he did, Theon had tossed his sword aside and tackled Sam to the ground, pinning him until he yielded.

Sam had been furious, and after Theon was walking away, Sam came after him. It had taken a group of other recruits to pull them apart. They were punished by clearing the latrines together. Slowly, as the evening had worn on, Sam had opened up, sharing his history and background. Something in him had made Theon want to trust him, and so he had shared his own story. From then on, every task, every drill, they had worked together. Their sparring sessions were just as heated, but they learned to adapt, punishing each other for their weaknesses. The day of the ceremony that accepted them into the guard, Sam had caught him just before they left, handing him a blade bound in cloth. Unwrapping it, Theon gripped a long, curved knife with a pale, bone handle.

Should the day come that your sword fails you and I am not by your side

Guilt welled up in him and he tried to turn from it, tried to repress it with the others, but somehow Alyce held it still. *He is a good man,* Alyce's voice commented.

Enough. You've seen what you need.

He sensed dismissal from her, but as he tried to pull away, he found himself trapped. When running did not work, he pushed back against her, shoving at her presence. *Enough,* he repeated. As he pushed, he felt the presence give, as though he had knocked a brick loose in a wall. Images suddenly flashed through his mind.

He was on a boat, long blond hair floating on the breeze. A boy was next to him, talking excitedly to his father, though it was not a man Theon recognised. The knowledge was there, though how he knew, he was unsure. The man was pulling at a sail and explaining something to them. Theon could not keep up, but pride and admiration soared through him.

Just as quickly as the image had come, it was gone. *What was that?*

He could sense embarrassment from Alyce, but she did not relent. *Who do you love?*

Sam appeared in his mind. As did Dhalia. To his surprise, so did Captain Islo, but when he questioned it, the memory of their first meeting came to him. Theon was in a cell, a boy curled in a ball against a wall. The door had screeched open, and the captain had stepped in. He took a seat on the bench and spoke to him. He was the first person to have spoken to him kindly in a long time. He told him not to waste his potential, not to throw away a future that Fate had offered him. The Captain had said to go with him, to use his energy to help people, and perhaps it was not too late to save him from a path Fate had not yet laid.

Theon tried to snatch himself away, but Alyce surrounded him. He felt as though he were bound in rope, and wriggling only moved the rope to a more uncomfortable position. Again, he pushed at her, trying to loose himself from her grip. He felt her slip, but before he could do more, memories consumed him again.

He was back on the boat. Dark clouds rumbled overhead and waves roared towards them, tossing the boat like a cat with a leaf. His father was fighting with a rope, shouting something to him. He stared to the boy, fighting to secure another knot, when he saw the wave. It towered over the boat and crashed down upon it, dowsing them in icy water. The boat was no longer under him, and he was unsure which way was up. He broke suddenly from underwater, gasping in mouthfuls of water. He shouted, but it was not his voice. It was a girl's. He called for his father, but water filled his mouth again, burning its way into his throat. He thought he saw the boy and tried to shout, tried to keep his head above water, but another wave turned the world black. The cold water swept his mind to blankness and he could feel himself sinking.

At first, there was desperation, but as he was tossed and sent spinning, resignation overcame him. As he fell deeper into darkness, he felt energy building in him as air rushed from his lips. Just as the world grew hazy, the thought of sand came to mind, a fading, fleeting thought of the shore, of a place of sanctuary.

Where are these memories coming from? he asked, his heart racing as he relived the scene.

Alyce's voice was strained, as though grappling to hold her grip, and the images were snatched away. *Cooperate, Theon. Where do you go from today?*

I-I don't know. I want to go south. I want to start again. Alyce, what were those visions?

She disappeared, and he was once more alone in his mind. He blinked, swaying at the sudden departure. His eyes were still trained on the candle. The wisp of smoke was trailing above the candle, curling before it disappeared. *Surely that's not the same smoke,* he thought, but he turned his attention to his own body. He felt oddly empty, as though something were missing. The energy, the vitality, it was gone, and without it, he felt barren. He shivered. In his hand, the ram burned.

Alyce handed him part of the biscuit as she crunched on her own. She eyed him carefully. He felt exhausted, surprised at the drain in his energy as he accepted the biscuit from her. 'What was that? Those memories, they weren't mine.'

She looked away from him. 'They were mine. It is as I said before: there were no secrets between us. One cannot ask a question without thinking of their own answer. I confess, I had not intended for such memories to rise, and I had not intended for you to see them.'

'That was you?' he asked incredulously. 'The girl was you? And that was your father?' Theon took another bite, surprised to find his hand shaking.

Alyce hesitated, then poured another glass of wine, broke off another piece of biscuit. 'And my brother. I lost them both that day. Perhaps seeing your bond with Sam reminded me of my own bond with my family. It is not a memory many would wish to see.'

'But you survived....'

She stared beyond him, to the black fabric of the tent over his shoulder. 'It was the day I discovered I was a Maxia. For many, it takes a trauma to release the magic. The last, dying scraps of energy are used in a final effort for self-preservation. What you saw is all I remember. Please, I do not wish to relive it again.'

Theon nodded, feeling some of his strength returned, but Alyce looked as though the ordeal had weakened her. 'Are you okay? I'm sorry I couldn't control myself.'

She chuckled. 'You did as everyone does. There are parts of us that we hide, especially from ourselves. There is plenty which we do not wish to see, and seeing them again is rarely pleasant. Anyway,' she said, setting the opened parcel aside, 'I must rest. Before I do, summon Jerrah. He waits outside.'

Theon stood, but his head swam and the tent tilted as though pitched on a hill. 'Slowly,' she cautioned him. He steadied himself, gripping the back of Alyce's chair.

He waited until his head cleared, then opened the flap to the tent. Sunlight and clean air poured in, forcing his eyes shut. *How is there still bright daylight? Surely I have been here hours.*

Two figures blocked out the light and stepped into the tent. One was Jerrah, the other was the lead rider from before, Mathias. 'Maxia,' Jerrah said, kneeling in front of Alyce. 'What'd you see? Is he who he says he is?'

She smiled. 'His name is not Perryn, but Theon. Aside from that, yes, he was a palace guard, and he wishes us no harm.' Theon felt some relief that that was all she said.

Mathias eyed Theon. 'He's with us?'

'Until your task is finished.'

He turned on his heel and swept the tent flap open, pausing there. 'Thank you, Maxia. Come with me, Theon. There is much to discuss.'

Theon looked back to Alyce, reluctant to leave her. Jerrah was helping her to the cot, but she called to Theon as he made to leave. 'Wear the pendent, deserter. I may need to contact you during your mission.' He was surprised to find it still in his hand. He nodded, not daring to defy a Maxia; he was still not sure he could trust her.

Mathias waited for him outside, and he started walking when he saw Theon, not waiting for him to catch up. Around them, tents stood like a forest. People watched as they passed, casting furtive glances and pausing in games of dice or conversation to see the newest addition to their camp.

'Jerrah's impressed,' he said gruffly. 'You can swing a sword, but you won't be going into the city looking for a fight.'

Theon frowned. 'What am I going in for? No one's told me what I'm supposed to be doing.'

'Later,' he dismissed. 'You've proven yourself with a blade, but you'll need something quieter. How are you with a bow?'

He shook his head. 'I'm better throwing a knife.'

The man frowned as they approached a circle of tents. In the centre, swords clashed and people sparred.

Off to the side, stuffed dummies were being filled with arrows. 'You'd throw away your weapon?'

'I'll still have my sword.'

'And if you have more than one target? Your task will require stealth—something a sword is not known for.' He led Theon to where arrows were fizzing through the air. A broad chested man noticed them and ambled over, thick veins pressed against his forearms.

'Mathias,' he greeted Theon's guide. 'Who've we got here? New recruit?'

'Not quite,' he said stiffly. 'Theon, this is our weapon master, Loit. He'll make sure you're ready.'

'I told you,' Theon tutted. 'I don't need a bow. Give me a knife and I'll do whatever it is you want.'

Mathias turned on him, narrowing his eyes. 'You're not in a position to argue, deserter. You'll use a bow, or I'll consider your agreement to help us revoked.'

Theon met his gaze, his jaw tightening. Loit nudged his arm. 'Come, lad. I'm sure I can teach you something.' He let himself be pulled away, though he could feel Mathias' stare burning between his shoulder blades. 'Ever used a bow?'

'Only as much as I've had to,' Theon said grudgingly.

Loit dipped his chin. 'Show me what've you got then.' He plucked a bow from a rack and handed Theon a quiver of arrows. Dummies were set at three different distances ahead of a wooden post. Theon gripped the bow, tested the tautness of the string. He pulled at it, letting the wood flex, before drawing an arrow. He held himself squarely, focussing on the nearest dummy. Relaxing his shoulders, he straightened his back, exhaled. On his next breath, he pulled the string to his chest. Peering along the arrow, he aimed slightly over the dummy, then loosed the arrow. The wood snapped back; the arrow leaped across the distance, skimming by the arm of the dummy and thumping into the leather sheet hanging behind it. Theon groaned inwardly.

'What were you aiming for, lad?' Loit looked at the dummy, retracing the trajectory of the missile.

'Heart,' he said stiffly, pulling another arrow from the quiver at his waist.

'Aim lower and consider the wind.'

'I know.'

'Then why didn't you? You only get one chance with a bow. Make it count.'

Theon repeated his process, shutting out his thoughts and ignoring Mathias as he watched from over his shoulder. This time, the arrow found itself in the belly of dummy. 'Too much,' Loit chided. 'Your adjustments should be minute. Focus.'

Again, Theon drew an arrow, taking less time to prepare himself. The arrow darted over the dummy's shoulder. Theon threw the bow to the floor. 'I told you, I'm not an archer.' He started to stalk away when Mathias blocked his path.

'Walk away and our deal is broken,' he warned.

'I don't even know what our deal is,' Theon cried. 'All I know, is that if I don't come with you, I'm a dead man.'

Mathias eyed him. 'Our deal requires you to be able to kill quietly and from afar. You need a bow.'

Theon's eyes flashed. He lunged for Mathias' belt, grabbing the knife from it. Before Mathias could react, Theon spun, flinging his arm out. The knife spun through the air, hilt over blade, until it embedded itself firmly in the head of the dummy. Several people stopped to stare.

'I *don't* need a bow,' Theon growled, shoving past Mathias and into the maze of tents.

Chapter X

Wind tussled his hair. The height of day had passed and in several hours the sun would be setting. Theon sat at the edge of camp, staring across the plains back to Corazin. *Why did I leave? I should have stayed with Sam and served my king. Now look at me, stuck with a band of rebels plotting to siege the city I grew up in.* He wondered if he could claim illness or report back with the rebel's plans in exchange for a pardon.

He knew it was futile. They would have his head before he could explain himself, and even if they let him speak, deserters scarcely live long.

His bundle landed next to him. 'I believe this is yours.' Theon grunted as Jerrah stood beside him. 'Think of it this way,' Jerrah said. 'Soon as this is done, you can carry on south. Put it all behind you and forget about it. Live your life as you see fit.'

Theon sighed. 'There's no forgetting this. It's one thing to break an oath you made to your king, another to act against him.'

He shrugged. 'You can start again. No one will know.'

'I'll know.'

'Not if you drink enough,' he grinned. 'I heard what happened on the training ground—sad to say I missed it. You have to teach me how to throw like that. They said you hit the target from twenty-five yards without even looking—and that Mathias' face was something to behold.'

Theon flushed. 'My temper got the better of me.'

'Not at all,' Jerrah said, taking a seat on the grass. 'You know what you're good at, and if you're better with a knife than a bow, then I don't see why you'd have to use a bow. It's your life on the line, mine too. I'd rather you had something that you could hit a target with.'

'So I don't need to use a bow?'

'Only if you tell me how to throw like you.'

'You want me to teach you?'

Jerrah nodded. 'Maybe once this is done you can show me. For now, instruction will be enough.'

Theon went through his process in his mind. He had first started throwing knives when he was a boy. After his mother had passed, he had earned scraps of food or a night's shelter by helping people that needed it, in any way he could. One of these was getting rid of the rats from inns, catching the ones the cats missed. The first time, an innkeeper had asked if he had ever done it before. 'Of course,' Theon had told him. He had convinced him that he was practically an expert, but he could only do it alone, and that it took a lot of patience.

Theon had not realised quite how much patience. He had tried waiting outside of their burrow, leaving crumbs and bait for them. Each time had they scampered out, he would try something new: hitting them with a broom, dropping a bucket on them, even throwing his shoe. Each time, he had been too slow, and the rat had something to fill its belly.

The innkeeper had fed him for his services, and while he ate, he had enquired about his successes. Theon had told him that it went well, but there was still one or two that were particularly evasive. When the innkeeper had asked to see how many he had caught, he told him that he had already fed the cats with them. Theon had retreated shortly after that to avoid any further questions.

He was sat on the floor in the room at the rear of the inn, picking his nails with a knife as he tried to come up with a new plan. A little brown smudge bounded into the edge of his vision and interrupted his musings. He forced himself to stillness. The rat had smelled the gravy and had made its way underneath the bed.

Moving slowly and fluidly, Theon weighed the knife in his hand, holding the blade between his thumb and finger. He turned slowly to face the bed, his plate between him and it. It was a game of waiting, to see who would break first. The rat lost. It crept out, nose high as it sniffed. Theon had wanted to move then, but he forced himself to wait until it was closer, to make it all the easier. Once the creature had convinced itself it was safe, it moved more directly. Theon forced himself to plan. Once he moved, the rat would try to flee. He tried to predict which way it would go. *Back to its nest,* he had guessed.

He drew in a breath, then moved. His hand whipped down from his shoulder and he released the knife. It rotated once, crossing the distance in a second. The rat had not the time to react. It found its mark, hit the rodent's hind flank. Theon leapt into the air, whooping in triumph. Only then did he see the creature still moving, squeaking in panic as it dragged its limp rear legs behind it. Theon rushed over and twisted its head.

Since then, it was a skill he had practiced regularly, swapping from the kitchen knife to a hunting knife. He had pilfered the keener blade from a man who had asked him to clear the bird's nest off of his chimney. Later, Theon had practiced with the bone-handled knife Sam had given him, and he could find his mark within an inch of where he was aiming.

Theon assessed the knowledge he had amassed over the years, then looked to Jerrah. 'First thing to get right is the rotation. It's no good throwing a blade as hard as you can when all it does it strike the target with the hilt, then hit the floor. Hold the knife between your thumb and the next joint up from your knuckle on your finger, like this.'

Jerrah copied Theon's hand and checked it was identical.

'Make sure the knife isn't touching the inside of your hand,' he corrected, 'otherwise you get this.' He turned his palm to show an array of tiny scars. 'After that, you need to stand up straight, relax your shoulders, and lift your hand so it's over your shoulder. You'll want to face your target straight on, then when you're ready, unfurl your arm and throw. It'll take a few tries to get right, but once you know your timing, it gets easier. Oh, and make sure you let go early enough, otherwise you'll be hopping to a healer to pull it out of your boot.'

Jerrah chuckled. 'Thank you, my friend. I shall practise before we leave.' He rose to his feet and offered his hand to him. 'Come, 'he said, 'it is time you learned your part in all of this.' Theon took a last look at the city before following Jerrah through the labyrinth of tents. As weaved through, Jerrah exchanged comments or nods to most of the troops on their route. Many were stirring, oiling mail or honing blades. An air of anticipation settled over the camp.

'They seem restless,' Theon observed.

'It's excitement, Theon. We're on the verge of change. The people know it and are eager to assert their power over the land, returning it to their kin.'

They approached a large tent, a castle in comparison to the stout structures surrounding it. Two armed men parted as they neared, pulling the flaps aside. Within, a large rectangular table took up the majority of the space with chairs dotted around it, most of them already filled. Mathias stood at one end of the table, hands clasped behind his back. Theon glanced at the other faces, most of them either avoiding him or burning gazes of distrust into his chest. It appeared they were late to the discussion, though Theon did not need to guess who had been at its core. Mathias nodded to them and waited until they were seated. The only other person Theon recognised was the Maxia.

Mathias cleared his throat. 'The end of our oppression is nigh,' he began. 'This time tomorrow, the monarchy will have succumbed to the power of the people, and Corazin will have a democracy. The people cry out for it, and we will give them their freedom. No longer will the powers sit, filling fat purses while mothers and babes starve on the streets.

'Earlier today, Fate gave us a gift. Theon, here, stumbled into our arms. He has agreed to aid our cause. Until this morning, he served as a palace guard. He knows the grounds better than any of us, and he knows the shifts of the guards and where they are posted. He is our greatest asset, and we will protect him duly.' He paused, letting his words settle. 'The Maxia has confirmed that Darrius has completed his role as figurehead. He has made a grave sacrifice for our cause, and tomorrow, when we sit in the Jade Hall, we will mourn with him. He is owed an unpayable debt. Do not let it be for naught.'

He leaned over the table, meeting the eyes of everyone at the table one by one. 'Five of you will go forth. You will meet the contact and enact the plan *exactly* as I tell it. The rest of the camp will follow, and the city will fall. There are some who have taken bribes and have arranged to not be at their stations tonight, but take no risks. This is our only chance.' Mathias took a seat and began detailing the plan to capture the king, thus relieving Corazin of its monarchy.

Theon ducked his head as they walked beneath the gates, hiding behind the side of his hood. He walked amid the rest of the team, disinterest or wonder on their faces. They were interspersed, avoiding walking as a group, but Theon doubted that he was ever out of their sight for more than a second. The guards on either side paid them no mind, passing them the barest of glances.

Inside, they exchanged a brief look, split into pairs, and dispersing down different roads into the city. They had entered through the western gate, taking a convoluted way into the city. Theon wore his cloak, disguising the sword at his belt as best he could. Two knives hung from the opposite side, neither by choice, weighing too much in the handle for his liking. It was either them or the bow, and he intended to use neither. 'A last resort' Jerrah had assured him.

Jerrah walked next to him, though whether he had volunteered to be paired with him or it was through planned monitoring, he was unsure. They pushed through the last of the crowds as the evening took hold, but Theon pretended he was new to the city, admiring the steep walls and bustling shop-fronts, studying the wares of every trader and merchant that called him over. He dropped his hood and soon began enjoying himself, appreciating the things that he had never seen as a man of the city. Instead, he became a traveller, letting everyone who called him over partake in his share of attention. He haggled and walked away, no matter the price he dragged them to, relishing that so many would fall to his refusal.

He had just left a tanner's, Jerrah long lost to the throng of people, when he looked ahead and spotted the parting crowds. Riding atop horses, two members of the palace guard swayed wordlessly, their gaze sweeping over those on foot. Theon recognised one of them and panicked. *Sam.*

He crossed the road and ducked into a shop, ignoring the herbs and rabbit's foot that hung from the rafters. The smell of wood shavings and lemon oil was thick in the air, but he turned to peer back through the warped glass, watching the distorted horses clop by. He sighed, leaning against the wall. *Too close,* he scalded himself.

'Just a moment,' a voice called from within the shop.

Theon rolled his eyes and shoved the door to the shop open. 'Sorry,' he mumbled, shouldering past a boy who made to enter. The politeness he had honed in his time with the guard was gone, sure that Jerrah would be looking for him. His companions had not tried to hide their distrust of him, and he wanted to do as little as possible to encourage a knife between his ribs.

Keeping his head low and his hood high, Theon weaved his way in and out of the streams of people, swerving to avoid the tray of a baker before slipping beyond the inner walls.

The streets were quieter closer to the palace, with jewellers and the more talented smiths and tanners already storing their wares for the night. A short walk later found him inside the *Burro Vago*, music and warm air spilling over him. He looked over the heads of those with their noses buried in their cup or engaged in conversation, spotting a pair sipping in the corner at a broad, round table. He went to the innkeeper, asked for an ale, and surveyed the room until the tankard thudded onto the counter. Theon slid his coin across the counter and made his way to the table, ignoring the man who plucked at a harp as he retold the tale of the *Dessius the Great*—one well-worn within these walls, but better received after recent events. It struck Theon as odd how opinion had changed so quickly. Years were seemingly forgotten, and minstrels only recited the days of the late-king's youth. In many of the inns in the outer ring, similar songs were recited, but they had not been for many seasons.

Theon nodded a silent greeting to the others, but took no part in their conversation, choosing instead to listen to their plans for life after that night. They spoke of a simple life, trusting that whatever was to come would be better than it was then. He soon grew bored of their fantasies and turned his attention to the minstrel. Those who performed in the inns beyond the outer walls we suggested to be of better talent, but their tales were often the same: some of legend, some of a mishap that befell an unlucky traveller, many of a beautiful maid and what was done to win her heart.

Theon drained his cup as Jerrah joined them. When Theon held his cup to a serving girl, she quickly replaced it with another. Jerrah smirked at him. 'Careful, my friend. You need a steady hand tonight.'

Theon raised his cup in acknowledgment. 'It's for a steady hand that I drink.' Only once darkness had settled outside did the final two trickle in, one with a new blade at his hip. Keen to show it to the others, he set it on the table for the others to pore over, admiring its finer details. The buyer revelled in the praise they gave it, and Theon resisted asking where he had procured it. He knew many a smith who could craft a fine looking sword, but when it came to combat, the blade would be no better than a one made of porcelain.

Together, they sat and spoke of what they had seen, most having never visited Corazin before, and Theon found he enjoyed the company, even if he rarely involved himself. They sat long into the evening, sipping at drinks, enjoying hot food and music. Some of them dreamt and laughed about the future, but despite himself, Theon sat uncomfortably. He smiled when the others did, but worried more than listened. The task ahead troubled him. It was more than just breaking his oath, more than just deserting. It was acting against those he had sought to serve, acting against those he had called brother. He resorted to sipping his ale, eyeing those occupying the tables around them as they laughed and joked with one another, wondering if they truly felt repressed, if a democracy was really what they longed for, or if Mathias and his army of rebels fought for an invented cause.

It was only after another round of drinks that another joined them. A boy, so young that Theon almost dismissed him as an apprentice of the inn. He climbed into a chair, ignoring the raised eyebrows as he greeted them. He slid a long key and a scrap of material across the table. 'Fourth on the right,' he said. 'If anything happens to her, Mr Kerrick will know—he's not a man you want to meet, especially not in a bad mood. He was once an assassin, or so the rumours say. He'll be of no concern once the night is through.' He took a swig from one of their tankards, swallowing deeply before leaving them to finish their own, his message delivered.

The men watched him go, disbelief on their faces. 'Am I dreaming, or did we just receive orders from a boy?' one said.

Jerrah shook his head. 'Those words weren't his—he's just a messenger. Our contact is within the council, but he refuses to meet personally until we are inside. He only works through others, but we can trust him.' The visitor had slowed their conversation, and when Jerrah stood, the others were quick to follow suit. Theon trailed after them as they stepped around tables, not drawing more than a sideways glance. They opened the door and left the music behind them.

The wind had redoubled its earlier efforts, kicking up a gale around them. The others talked between one another, walking in a huddle and joking as though they were simply on their way home from the inn, but Theon knew it was a disguise for nerves.

They made their way to a separate inn, several minutes' walk from the one they had come from. They filed in and Jerrah nodded to the innkeeper behind the counter. They spoke quietly, and if a pouch of coin was passed, Theon did not see. 'Three rooms at the end of the corridor,' he said to them. 'Good luck, lads,' he added in a hushed voice. Theon grimaced, wondering how many others new of their scheme.

They thudded up a narrow staircase and Jerrah sheparded them into a room, closing the door behind him. 'Settle down for a few hours. You'll need your rest. I'll fetch you when the time's right. Leave all of your belongings here, swords too. We'll collect them after.' There was a murmur around the room, then a pair of them left, as did Jerrah, and Theon followed after him. Jerrah was already inspecting the bed when he walked in. 'Probably a good thing I'm not sleeping in this thing. Riddled with bugs.'

Theon rolled his eyes, dropped his belt beside the bed, and plucked a knife from it, weighing it across his palm. It was heavier in the handle than the one Sam had given him, the blade shorter, but it was sharp, and that was not lost on him. Tucking it under the pillow, he threw the duvet over himself and rested his head, letting his breathing slow. *This might be the last night I get in a decent bed for a while, might as well make the most of it.* He turned and faced the wall, eyeing the window and the night beyond. Behind him, a candle flickered, casting shadows across the wall as a scraping sound came from a whet stone against a blade.

'How long had you been serving?' Jerrah asked, lovingly passing the stone along his sword.

'Two summers,' he said, not turning.

'And you've never seen a battle? Never seen a death?'

Theon shrugged. 'Only executions—the king's justice. Arrested a couple of drunks, punched a few more in the face, nothing much.'

Jerrah nodded. 'I'm sorry, you know, but in a way, you should be grateful. Fate has chosen you. Better to be on our side than theirs.'

Theon turned, sitting up. 'They are good men, Jerrah. How many have to die? They serve the crown, not the boy that wears it.'

He paused. 'There will be as many as those who stand in our way.' Theon looked on, and Jerrah set the whet stone aside with a sigh. 'I can't guarantee the safety of your friends, Theon. They may not wear the crown, but they are the threat. We are one side of a battlefield, they are another. I wish it weren't so, but Fate has laid its path. All we may do now is tread upon it.'

Theon curled his lips in disgust. 'What is it with you people and your trust in Fate? I was only asked to show you the way.' He threw himself onto his side, his back to Jerrah. 'I won't kill the men I trained with.'

'I don't expect you to. I was in your position, once. Those men are your brothers.' There was a silence, and Theon hoped that was the end of the conversation, but Jerrah spoke again, his voice soft. 'I first met Darrius in Oreth. I was stood on a platform, the auction well under way. The bidding had starting quickly, as it always does. I was nothing special, but I was young, and I could work, so perhaps that made me valuable. It was only as the bidding slowed that it dawned on me that one of the two men who shouted would take me away, that I would have to do whatever they ordered. One bid something high, and crowd fell to a hushed murmur. It was out of this silence that Darrius doubled it. He caused an uproar, but I was sold immediately. I was dragged away as soon as the gold left his hand.

'We walked for a time and he said nothing. I wondered why he had bought me, and for such a sum, but the worry of my chores soon overtook this, guessing only the worst. Without any warning, he stopped and pulled me into an alley, taking me by the shoulders. "You're free, now," he told me. He said I had a choice. I could go with him, a free man. I would have food and shelter, I would work for him, and be rewarded for it. Or I could walk. I could resume my life and wait until I was captured again, sold to someone else less favourable. I didn't believe him, you know. I thought it was a test, but something made me stay.

'He was good to his word. He sheltered me, cared for me, and taught me my swordsmanship. He'd say that he was once a knight, once a great man, and I would laugh and say that I had been too. I didn't know the truth of his words, and why would I? He didn't wear gold or finery. He looked like everybody else, maybe with a scar or two more. We travelled along the southern coast, stopping where he chose, and in each town he would arrange to meet someone, disappear for hours, and when he returned in the evening, he brought a pouch heavy with gold. I never knew what he did, but he would only wink at me and tell me that questions were dangerous things.

'One day we were staying in Lura. We'd arrived that morning and were looking for a market. Well, we found one. Darrius knew my reaction before I did. He gripped my wrist, holding me back from launching myself into the bidding and cutting the poor souls free. He told me to wait, and so we did. I watched as men and women were sold. Every shape, size, and colour. Some were sold for great fortunes, others were sold for scraps. All of them, we watched. Once the pen was empty and the platform clear, the crowds began to leave. "It's too late," I had told him, "they're all leaving." Still, he told me to have patience. I watched as they were dragged away, most too riddled with despair to fight back as they were lost to the streets of the city. It made me wonder what my life would have been like had Darrius not been there to pay for my freedom.

'We waited until a man started walking away, a man following with a chest in his arms. It had a shining lock on it, and the man behind seemed to struggle with its weight. "Him," Darrius told me, and we set off after them. We followed until the roads were quiet, then, when only a few people were around, Darrius leaped forward, not giving me any warning. Darrius killed the man with the box, and I struck at the merchant, hamstringing him. He fell with a cry, but men surrounded us, clustering from unseen shadows. Six of them, all with swords. They weren't guards, though. They were bought-men, like I had been. "Go," Darrius had told them. "You're free now—your only loyalty is to yourself." The man on the floor shouted at them, hurled insults at them and ordered that they protect him.

'That's the problem with bought protection, you see. It's only as loyal for as long as it has to be. Two of them threw down their swords and ran, another made to attack Darrius, but Darrius was too quick. The remaining three turned on their master, opening his throat onto the street. They opened the box, took what they could, and thanked us.

'I thought that was it, but they remained a moment, seemingly unsure of what to do or where to go. Then one turned and said that if he'd have them, they wished to pay their debt to Darrius. He insisted that there was no debt, but they remained, and so we continued.'

Jerrah was quiet for some time, and Theon wondered if he were reliving those seasons. 'It was not always as easy as that, though. For many, their lives were so broken. Their masters had splintered their souls and crippled their bodies, and though they were my brothers, I did what was kindest, so they might suffer no longer. I know what it is you fear, Theon, and no blood need be spilled by your blade. But know this,' he paused, the floorboards creaking under him as he leaned forward. 'You act against my brothers, and I won't hesitate.'

Theon stole the duvet across him tighter. Life south sounded harsh and wild, and Theon wondered at all that might have happened to Jerrah between then and now. He thought that, if circumstance had been different, they might have been friends. He might have even stayed and travelled with him, but he knew they would stay in Corazin for a time, and Theon could not linger. *My life is not here. Not anymore.*

'Say, Theon, you never said, where do you hope to go after tonight? What lies ahead for you?'

He grimaced. 'You said Fate has laid its path. I can only go where it leads me.'

Theon heard Jerrah's smile. 'Ah, but that was not the question. Where you hope to go might not be where you end up, but it is still nice to know where the heart would take you if it could.'

'South. I'll find some wealthy merchant or a vineyard, offer my protection. It'll be a simpler life.'

'And one you'll grow fat on. You'll do well for yourself, my friend.'

He snorted. 'You've known me a day. Unless you're a soothsayer, I'll go south until somewhere convinces me to stay. It might be the ocean, it might be the mountains. Who knows, maybe it'll be a woman. Until then, I'll walk until something tells me otherwise.' He took a breath and exhaled. *After tonight. Once this night is over, I'll be free, and this city will be behind me.*

Chapter XI

A hand shook his shoulder and the knife was free of the bedding in an instant. He rolled onto the floorboards, knees bent, arms poised. Jerrah stood on the other side of the bed, bemused. 'If I wanted you dead, you wouldn't have woken up.' He shook his head, smiling. 'Bloody soldiers, thinking nought else but brute force'll save their lives. Come, my friend. It's time. I'll wake the others.'

Theon nodded, walked to the wash bowl and splashed his face. He felt calm, and guilty for feeling it. He watched the water ripple for a moment, letting it settle. *I won't see him. He'll be fine.*

He strapped his belt around his waist, tightened his boots, and made his way down to the common room of the inn. The fire was low in the hearth, kicking out a haze of warmth. The innkeeper was wiping down tables, all of them empty, and Theon wondered how old the night was. He focussed on keeping his mind clear.

Several minutes later, boots tramped down the steps. The innkeeper raised an eyebrow, leaving them with a nod of encouragement.

'Ah, Theon,' Jerrah said, 'thought you'd run off on us.'

'I've broken my word enough recently.'

He raised an eyebrow and gestured to the door. 'Then lead the way, my friend. We're with you.'

Theon lifted his hood and stepped into the night. The bluster had not subsided, carrying with it a chill that forced its way inside his clothes, but he did his best to ignore it. Instead, he focussed on which route would be less likely to encounter any patrols. Leading them through the streets, they wound their way past shuttered windows, the occasional drunk or stray dog the only ones to notice their passing. Instead of walking along the wall, Theon chose to navigate from several houses away, keeping an eye on the walls. The palace sat as the centrepiece of the city, perched atop a hill to stand in grandeur over all that basked in its shadow.

Theon lifted a hand, and the group huddled around. 'There's a guardhouse ahead. We won't be able to pass without being noticed. If I go alone, I might be able to distract them for long enough.'

'I'll go with you,' Jerrah said, setting off ahead of him, 'in case you need help.' Theon hurried to catch up, but Jerrah kept his voice low. 'You have a plan?'

'Walk in and see what happens.'

'Don't ever become an officer, Theon.'

They strode up to the gate, light pooling out from the window of a small hut attached to it. Theon already knew the layout of the room: a small square table in the centre, a candle on top of it and a game of cards well underway. One of the men would have their back to the window, the other facing it, keeping an eye out for any movement beyond. After the king's assassination, more had been put on shift, but the northern gate was the quietest. Any travellers or merchants would use the southern and eastern gates; the northern gate led to the road into the Hackles.

They paused outside of the door to the guardroom. Theon guessed that they could have easily sneaked past, but not knowing where the patrols were could lead to one marching up right behind them. Theon dropped his hood, gripped the handle, and took a breath. Theon threw the door open and stumbled inside. 'Come, quick. Rebels are at the gates.'

The two guards sat dumbfounded for a moment. One was older, a man Theon knew had served his entire life. The other was a summer recruit. Their swords were leaning against the wall, cards blown out of position.

'Theon?' the younger said, twisting in his chair. 'But... rumours are you'd ran off? What happened?'

'There's no time,' Theon urged, stepping inside. 'Let's go.'

The younger opened his mouth to reply, but an arrow sprouted from his forehead, interrupting him. The older man yelled, scrambling for his sword. 'Theon, watch out.' As he laid his hand on its hilt, an arrow pierced his ear and lodged in his skull. Both men hit the floor with a thud.

Theon whirled. 'What the *fuck* was that?'

Jerrah plucked another arrow from his quiver. 'You were about to send them running down the road and past the others. They'd have died anyway.' He signalled to the rest of their group as Theon stared at the bodies before him. Blood gleamed in the candlelight and he steadied himself on the back of a chair. Jerrah hesitated. 'Are you okay, my friend? They're sacrifices for the people of Corazin. You knew this was coming.'

Theon swallowed and nodded, not wanting to look anywhere. He felt a hand slap his shoulder.

'Then come, let us free our kingdom.'

The others shuffled into the room, crowding it. 'Where next?' one of them asked.

Jerrah looked to Theon, who took a shaky breath. 'We can either wait until the patrol comes to replace their shift,' he said, gesturing to the guards, 'or leave them and go ahead.'

'How long until the shift change?'

'No way to tell. It works on a relay system. If it's just changed, we have an hour. The game looks well-underway,' Theon nodded to the remaining cards, 'so probably less.'

Jerrah pushed the door open again. 'Then let's hope Fate has a clear path ahead.'

They skulked across the palace grounds, ears strained for any sound mingled in with the wind. Theon kept as far from the building as possible, following along the shadow of the walls. After a quick glance, they broke their cover and he led them across the southern courtyard before coming to the kennels. Conversation floated from the kitchens, but no one moved beyond the candlelight. Theon nodded to the others and crept inside the kennels, pausing to let his eyes adjust.

No lights shone in the drafty shelter, but stepping out of the worst of the wind was a relief. A whimper came from the other side of the aisle, but he paid it no mind. Instead, he walked along the stalls, counting the hinges as he went. *One, two, three.* He stopped at the fourth and slid the lock back, leading with a strip of dried meat. A wet nose touched his hand and the venison was snatched from his fingers. The nose returned a moment later for more. Theon smiled, pleased to be greeted by a wagging tail. Jerrah joined him in the stall and crouched, rubbing the dog behind the ear. 'This her?'

'Must be,' Theon whispered, 'she's the only one in here.' He heard Jerrah move and the dog snuffed at something. Jerrah tied the scrap of cloth around the collar, a leash already tied to it. They stood, and the dog pulled him through the kennels, excited by the midnight adventure. They met the others at the door, continuing into the night.

Theon guided the group back across the courtyard and towards the palace gardens, but a hand grabbed his sleeve, jerking him back behind a wall. Jerrah pressed a finger to his lips and peered around the corner. Two soldiers walked ahead, talking quietly. *Shift change,* Theon realised. 'We don't have long,' he said in a hushed voice. Jerrah took no time to hesitate. He stepped out from behind the wall, bent onto one knee, and drew an arrow back. Before he could loose it, Theon grabbed his arm, pushing the bow down. Jerrah shrugged him off and other hands pulled him back, but before Jerrah could draw the arrow again, the guards turned a corner, and strolled out of sight.

'What are you playing at?' Jerran hissed.

Theon glared at him. 'You said no one would die needlessly.'

'No? Now they're going to walk back, one change closer to finding the two in the guard house.'

'And what of the guards before that? Those expecting their change, and no one turns up? This gives us longer.' Theon did not wait to see if his argument convinced them. He stole across the gardens to a stout, stone building. The door was made of a heavy wood, and Theon had never seen it open, nor even known it could. As far as he had been aware, it was an ancient mausoleum, used by the royal family until several generations ago, when the deceased were laid to rest in unknown crypts hidden in the mountains. As Theon understood it, the building served a purely ornamental purpose now. He glanced about. 'Are you sure this is where we have to go?'

Jerrah said nothing. He slid the key into the lock, a clank as he turned it answering his question. The door squealed open, making the group cringe. Jerrah quickly ushered them down a cold set of narrow stairs and into darkness, the door closing firmly behind them. The air was stale and musty, and Theon wondered who the last people had been to walk there. There was a moment of confusion and hushed mumbles as they made sure they were all together and facing the right direction as they shuffled into the darkness.

It was the dog who led them, sniffing and trotting. The humans trailed, hands on shoulders in a train. Without any light, all other senses became heightened, and Theon was sure the scuff of a boot would alert everyone to their presence.

The longer they walked, the more Theon realised that there was much of the palace than he had never patrolled. He wondered at the purpose of such a network of tunnels, and how far they spread. Suddenly, the dog barked, making Theon jump, its voice echoing several times over. He felt Jerrah's shoulder tense, resisting against the pulling of the hound.

'Shut that thing up,' a man behind him cursed, but Jerrah's step only quickened.

'She's got a scent.' Jerrah tightened his grip on the leash and they followed, trusting their guide to avoid walking into walls despite the occasional stumble. Light glowed in a rectangle ahead of them. They gathered in front of it, sharing nervous looks as they collected themselves. The dog whined and scraped its claws against the wood. Theon heard someone take a breath, then a rapid sequence of knocks. For a moment, the only sound was their breathing, then a clunk came. The door opened and light flooded into the chamber, forcing Theon to squint and lift a hand to shield his eyes. A warm wave of air washed over them and a withered face scowled at the group.

'You're late, and hardly quiet—the whole palace could have heard that dog.'

Theon was sure he recognised him. He was frail, with papery skin that looked like aged leather. He had bright eyes and he wore a night gown.

Jerrah blinked. 'Lord Serril?'

The old man regarded him. 'Are you dead yet?'

Jerrah bristled but let it go. 'There was a problem getting in without being seen. It's dealt with, but we don't have much time.'

The man nodded, surveying the group. He frowned. 'There was only meant to be five of you. Who's the extra?'

'Last minute recruit,' Jerrah said shortly, stepping out of the corridor. 'Knows his way onto the grounds, and without him, we wouldn't have gotten here.'

The man narrowed his eyes, and suddenly Theon recognised him. 'You were at Darrius' audience this morning.'

The man raised his eyebrow. 'And apparently so were you. Jerrah, are you sure you trust this man? He has served his purpose and he would not be the only sacrifice this city has to make tonight.'

Jerrah shot him a look. 'The Maxia says he can be trusted. We've made a bargain, and he has kept to his word. I intend to keep mine.' He nodded to the dog tugging at the leash, whimpering impatiently. They had surfaced from a hidden door into a library. Theon marvelled at how well the brick hid the door once it closed. He had never been inside the library before: it was considered private quarters, and there was no need for protection within.

Serril moved into the room, slipping silently over rugs as though his feet never touched them. He paused by a table and waited for them to join him before speaking in a quiet voice. The dog tugged at the leash. 'Before I can draw Raiden here, the Última Sombra need to be taken care—'

'The what?' one of the men asked.

'The king's personal guard,' Serril dismissed. 'Beyond those doors, two corridors join. To the right, a corridor leads to a door and a guard. Directly ahead, another opens out into an audience chamber. The first door on the right is the king's. I have ensured that his guard is absent for a time. Another corridor joins from the left, farther up. There is a guard stood by the queen mother's chambers. He must be dealt with. Do not harm the queen, if it can be helped. She still has her uses. We have until the attack on the city is launched. After that, our window of opportunity will slam shut and the guard will triple. Jerrah, assign your men.'

Jerrah looked between them, nodding. 'Leon, Timas, take the door straight on from here. Petor, Lan, go with Serril. You'll dispatch the guard outside the queen's door, then again outside the door of that corridor. Serril will wait until the corridors are clear, then summon the king to the library. Theon, you'll come with me. We'll take the last man then wait until Serril walks with the king to the library. Soon as I see the king, I'll loose the dog and complete the mission.'

'Remember,' Serril cautioned, 'it must look like the boy is mauled. It must look like the beast-master is involved.'

Jerrah cast a final look across the group, nodding, then led them to the door. 'Good luck, brothers. May you all see dawn.'

The door creaked open and the group dispersed. Theon stepped into the hall, but Jerrah caught his shoulder. 'Let the others go first.' They watched the others slip into the torchlit hallways, the sound of feet shifting through the corridor whispered back to them. Theon peered ahead as the group paused at the junction. There was a moment of silence, then one of them stepped out. Theon was unsure of what happened, but a shout went up. The group suddenly pressed themselves against the wall as a voice shouted for a man to show himself. As soon as the man rounded the corner, four bodies jumped him. There was a brief struggle, then silence. They waited, listening, and when nothing more came, two disappeared to the left and the remaining two continued on. Theon squinted into the gloom, thought he saw a glimpse of light at the end of the hallway, then it disappeared as he blinked. Serril waited, poised outside of the king's door.

'Here,' Jerrah said, handing Theon the leash. 'I'll do what must be done, just keep out of the way.'

They started down the corridor, but the dog pulled the opposite way, whining louder. 'Come on,' he hissed, tugging it after Jerrah. Half way down the corridor, it barked in frustration, making him jump.

'Keep it quiet,' Jerrah snapped, but before he could, it barked again. Theon clamped his hand around the dog's muzzle. It fought and wriggled, growling. The dog seemed in a frenzy, possessed.

A sound came from the door at the end of the passage, then Theon heard voices from around the corner also. Jerrah broke into a sprint, charging towards the door. Theon fought the dog, straining to see who came through the door. He spotted the blonde hair, and his heart sunk. The dog gave a last pull and the leash tore from his fingers, but Theon let it go hurtling down the corridor, baying frantically.

Theon chased after Jerrah. He had dropped to a knee, drawn the string back, and Theon could only watch as he loosed an arrow, letting it hum through the air. A thud came from down the corridor and Sam recoiled. The arrow thumped into the wooden door frame, a hand's width from his face. He stared at it for a moment, startled.

'Move,' Theon shouted. Sam blinked, then retreated behind the door, unsheathing his sword. Jerrah threw his bow down, but before he could reach for his dagger, Theon crashed into him, sending them both sprawling. Jerrah sprang to his feet, advancing as Theon scrambled to his feet. 'I knew you couldn't do it,' he snarled. 'You betrayed your king, now you betray me. Your word is dirt, deserter.'

A voice shouted from behind him, but Theon faced Jerrah. He knew his speed and knew the slightest invitation would result in a knife in his neck. Somewhere, a boy yelled, and behind Jerrah, Theon saw a body tumble to the ground, the hound on top of it.

'You can't stop us, deserter,' Jerrah taunted. 'Fate has already set its path for the city. You've only delayed your death.'

Theon kept himself low, ready to spring in attack or retreat in defence. 'Isn't that what we're all after? A little bit longer? Come, Jerrah, why delay yours any further?'

Jerrah snarled and leapt forward. Theon ducked to the side, barely seeing the blade as it flashed in the torchlight. A fist lodged itself in his stomach, driving the air out of him and doubling him over. 'Big guys like you can't do shit in a brawl,' Jerrah hissed. 'Too big, too slow.'

The rebel jumped to the side of him and Theon heard the clash of metal. Sam had his sword drawn, Jerrah dancing away from it. A snarl came from the library doors, but none of them paid it any notice.

'Here,' Sam said, not taking his eyes off of Jerrah. 'This is yours.'

Theon tossed the heavy knife he had been given aside, taking the bone-handled blade from Sam. His fingers curled around the handle, the bone fitting comfortably into the groove of his palm.

'Together,' Sam said, crouching.

Theon did not wait. He lunged, leading with his free hand. He deflected Jerrah's first strike, letting the knife in his other hand drive towards the man's gut. Jerrah managed to turn, the blade only cutting at his jerkin. He gave Theon a shove, using his momentum to propel him further. In one swift motion, Jerrah ducked, dodging the swinging sword that sliced over his head as Sam charged forward. Jerrah took two paces back, and once more they were stood at a stand-off. Theon climbed to his feet.

'Enough,' Jerrah snapped. A menacing twinkle shone in his eye. 'You know, you're right, Theon. A bow isn't as good as a knife.'

Before Theon could react, Jerrah flicked his wrist, sending a dagger spinning through the air. It came to a stop, accompanied by a grunt. Sam stumbled back, eyes wide, his sword dropping to his side. He stared at the knife protruding from his chest before his knees buckled.

Theon moved. He swooped down, plucking the sword from the ground, and advanced on Jerrah.

'What you going to do, deserter? It's over. Run. Go south and hide like a kitten.'

Theon snarled, slicing the sword towards Jerrah. He watched him, knowing he had only one chance. At the last second, Theon pivoted and changed his direction. He let his own momentum lift him off his feet into a roll before springing up behind Jerrah. He thrust the sword through his ribs, feeling the metal grate against bone. A hoarse gasp came from Jerrah as Theon stood behind him. 'And I learned a thing or two from you.'

He let he sword go, and the body dropped. Theon skipped over it, rushing to Sam's side. His eyes were already distant, but they found Theon's face. 'You came back.'

'Couldn't just leave you, could I?'

A woman's voice interrupted him, calling from somewhere around the corner. 'Raiden!' It was the queen.

Sam glanced down the corridor to the library. The boy was scrambling to his feet, but the dog snapped at his ankles, tripping him. The dog was on top of him as he fought to keep the snapping jaws at bay, though Theon could see even from a distance he had not been successful previously. Sam struggled, trying to lift himself, the panic on his face clear. 'Save the king, Theon.'

'No, I can save you.' He pulled at his arm, trying to hoist him up, but Sam refused. 'The king, Theon. You swore an oath.' Theon faltered and Sam took his hand and pressed it to his chest, tightening Theon's fingers around the pale-hilted blade. 'Go.'

Theon looked up to see the dog snarling over the boy. It jerked back, gripped his arm in his mouth and shook its head as the boy kicked at it. Theon knew the battle was already lost. He looked back to Sam, watched as the fight slipped out of him and his breath shallowed. There was no coming back.

Anger bubbled in Theon's chest. He threw himself to his feet and sprinted down the hallway, knife in hand. The dog drew itself back, poised in a crouch, and the boy tried to use the moment to retreat, dragging himself back, leaving his chest and neck exposed. Anger raged through his mind, shoving aside any rationale.

Heat suddenly flared from his chest, making him stumble. The ram pendent around his neck burned against his skin. Words sounded in his mind, passing as swiftly as that of thought. *Choose wisely, deserter. You act for the good of your city, now. You've seen the monster. Is that a man who can care for your homeland?*

Alyce?

Who else? Theon, Fate is at a crossroads, and the path this city takes lies with you. Will vengeance be enough? You still deserted those you vowed to serve. A dead dog won't change that, nor will it bring back your friend.

You're on their side.

The presence enveloped his mind and he was suddenly blinded by the energy that held his mind. *I serve the people of this land. If I was on their side, would I have sent you with them? I could have had you executed after you left my tent. This is your decision, but know this: if the king survives, he will not rest. He will spend his wrath hunting all those who oppose him. You may seek peace, but he will never abandon his search. War bubbles in a cauldron, it is up to you whether it boils over. Choose wisely, deserter.*

The presence was gone, and he was once more in control of his body. The conversation had occurred in mere seconds and Theon blinked as he returned his attention to the scene. He skidded to a halt as the dog reared in front of the boy. *How can she know the future? I took an oath, and my king needs me.*

Theon's arm shot through the air, just as the dog lurched forward. He turned, not waiting for the blade to find its mark. A high-pitched yelp sounded as he turned for the door. He ripped the pendant from around his neck and tossed it to the side as he ran.

To the gates. It's time I left this city behind me. These walls have caged me long enough.

Theon rushed through the palace, ignoring shouts and startled looks. He threw the doors open and stepped into the night.

It is time I was a free man.

The Apprentice

Chapter XII

The cart rattled beneath him, and he was glad to be off of his feet. Two horses plodded in front, heads bobbing as they walked. He rummaged in the pack between his feet and pulled a waterskin from within, taking a long draught. The merchant shook his head when offered, declining it with a smile. The stranger had a thick waist and a wobbling belly, but his smile was as broad as his hair was thin. 'Keep it. You look like you need it more than I do. What's your name, traveller? You look like you've not seen four walls and a hot meal for too many nights.'

His stomach growled, and he grinned. 'You could say that, mister. Name's Eder, but you can call me Ed.'

'Trast,' he said, nodding a greeting of his own.

'Thanks for stopping, Trast.'

He chuckled. 'If I hadn't stopped, you'd have tripped over your own feet. What's taking you to Corazin?'

'Work,' the boy said, settling back into the wooden bench with a sigh. The morning was clear, if windy. Some folk travelled the roads, but they were few and far between. In every direction, only open plains and swooping birds accompanied them. To the north, woodlands stretched towards the O'Pasos and the Hackles, and he marvelled at them, amazed at how the mountains only seemed to grow higher and higher, a white layer capping their peaks. Behind it, the pale, blue sky seemed delicate, something he had only seen since beginning his travels and rising with the sun. *Grand Pa had been right, going around them may have taken longer, but at least I have all my toes.*

Trast looked at him out of the corner of his eye, eyebrow raised. 'Work? Forgive me, lad, but you don't look like you've yet learned a trade.'

Eder smirked. 'I haven't. It's what brings me here.'

'You've got my respect for that,' he nodded. 'Apologies for my prying, but could you not follow your father's trade?'

'My father's the one who sent me away,' Eder said. 'I'm the youngest of four. Pa's workshop was crammed enough, and my brothers haven't yet finished their training. He's got no more time, so he sent me on my way. Said to learn a trade that our village needs and make a living for myself.'

'Your father sent you on your own?'

He nodded. 'Gave me this pack and his blessings, then sent me on my way.'

'Well, lad, whatever you do, don't go into the lumber trade. It's hard work and you never get the splinters out.'

'I'll bear that in mind,' he grinned.

Trast sighed, giving the reins a flick. 'So, Corazin is ahead of us, but you look like you've come far. What's behind you?'

'Haystacks and bushes, mostly. Started off from Croner. Since then, I've worked where I could for food or a space in a barn. Where I couldn't, my shelter was under stars and branches.'

Trast's jaw tightened. 'Croner, the fishing village? You've come that far?'

Eder shrugged, 'I guess so.' He wished there was more to the land instead of grass and the occasional farm. Grand Pa had told him tales of the world, told him about the tallest mountains and the deepest canyons. So far, his own journey had little more than irritable farm folk and dusty roads. 'Why aren't there more farms around? Surely these plains could be farmed?'

'Ah, a merchant, are you? The land is too tough. There's a reason that only the grass grows on the Great Plains of Corazin. Those who farm here only grow hardy crops and have done for generations. They have learned from their fathers and grandfathers, and whatever secrets they harbour, they are loath to part with them. It's a harsh land at the best of times, but why Corazin? Haven't you heard? The king's been assassinated, and rebels are camping on the city's doorstep.'

Eder chuckled. 'If I listened to every rumour that the king had been killed, I'd have believed that there had been twenty kings in my time alone. It's nonsense.'

'It's true,' Trast turned to face him, leaning closer, as though someone in the empty landscape might overhear. 'Killed by magic, they say. Pulled his blood from his eyes and his bones from his skin. That's what they say, lad, and I believe it. If you ask me, I'm just glad they didn't stick around. Don't like the idea of Maxia running about the countryside.'

Eder looked at him. 'You believe in magic?'

'Didn't used to, but after this? How can a man not?'

'Well,' he said, relaxing, 'I'll believe it when I see it.'

'Aye, and for your sake, I hope you don't. Where there's magic, there's only pain to come. Fate skews off its path where magic's concerned.'

Eder nodded thoughtfully. He had heard similar from the few who had chosen to speak to him on; not one of them had wanted anything to do with magic.

'So, Ed. Where are you going to look for work? Got anywhere you want to go?'

'The palace,' he said without a moment's hesitation.

The driver jolted in surprise. 'The palace? Why'd you want to work there? That's no trade, lad.'

'Perhaps,' he shrugged, 'but I'm looking for a man. Only he can teach me.'

'And what's that? There are plenty of people in the city. Go into any inn and half the folk there could teach you something.'

Eder shifted as a wheel ducked into a hole and bounced them out again. Trast glanced back over his shoulder, making sure his load remained unshifted. 'Only one man can teach me this. It's… an old art.'

'Ah, an art? Like a poet? Or a minstrel?'

He smiled again, tilting his head. 'Something like that.'

'Well, I hope you find whoever it is you're looking for.' He sat up, peering along the road before pointing. 'You see that, lad?' Eder sat forward and squinted. 'That'd be your first glimpse of Corazin. Another hour or so and her walls will be looming high in front of us.'

Trast's word was true. The horses had soon tugged them to the outskirts of the walls. The road had become increasingly populated as the morning had grown older, though Eder was unsure whether this was because they were closer to the city or that some had simply had the fortune of a longer rest than he. These thoughts were soon brushed aside as he began to understand the vastness of the city: he was sure that if part of the walls toppled, the entire of Croner could be squashed beneath it. On his journey he had passed through other villages and towns, admiring how they had spanned outwards and life seemed to culminate in the centre, but Corazin was on another scale. The comparison reminded him of a trader's galley next to a dinghy. He peered up and thought he saw a head peered over the ramparts. *I must look no bigger than a beetle from up there,* he thought with a smile.

'If you ever get the chance, go to Pevon.' Trast said, noticing his expression. 'It's twice as large, and it's a damn sight warmer.'

The wind tussled the horse's manes, but Eder took no notice. He stared at the gates, awestruck at the size of the portcullis and the brick work, thinking each brick must be several times heavier than he was. *If anyone were to attack the city, they'd do well just to breach the walls.* Guards stood on either of the gate but neither paid them any more attention than a side-eyed glance at the cart and its contents. Once beyond the gates, Eder was stunned by the amount of people that milled about. There must have been nearly the same amount of people on this road as in the whole of Croner. Noise and wares moved around them, no one noticing them save to avoid being trampled.

Eder shivered. With so many people all talking or shouting to one another, he felt suddenly alone. He knew no one, and he doubted help would come freely. Panic fluttered in his chest, and for the first time since he had left, he longed to turn around. He was sure he could convince Pa to take him back, to promise to never again give him reason to disown his son. Even as he thought it, he knew it was foolish There was no going back, and if his father ever saw him again, Eder doubted it would be with kind words and an embrace.

Buildings stood shoulder to shoulder, stacked on top of one another, taller than he had ever seen. Most of the houses had windows above the lowest set, and sometimes there were even windows above these.

A hand clapped his shoulder, drawing him back to the swaying cart. 'Well, lad, what do you think?'

'It's... big.'

Trast laughed, his belly wobbling. 'Aye, lad, that it is. I'm afraid it's time we part ways, but here, take this.' He held out a small pouch of coin. He pressed it into Eder's hand. It was light, but he was stunned by the kindness.

'For-for what? I don't understand?'

'For keeping me company, and so you can find yourself a proper meal, eh?'

Eder accepted it, tucking it into a pocket on the inside of his jerkin. 'Thank you, Trast,' he said, stepping down from the cart. 'Truly.'

'Think nothing of it, and hey, once you've mastered your trade and looking for wood to build your home, be sure to find me.'

Eder smiled. 'I will, I promise.'

'Good lad. May your path be true and your journey clear.' He flicked the reins and Eder watched as the cart became lost in the ever-shifting tide of bodies.

He touched his hand to his breast, feeling the weight of the coin hidden there. Adjusting his pack, he set off. *What's the rush?* he thought. *I have all the time in the world. Perhaps I'll just explore for a time, have myself a hot meal, and then make my way to the palace, wherever it may be.*

So he wandered, going wherever his feet pleased, content to admire the wares of any merchant that caught his attention. At first, he stopped at every voice that called to him, but after several he realised it would be nightfall before he found his was beyond that first street.

One of the things that amazed him most was the noise. Shouts came from everywhere; metal crashed against metal and hammers pounded nails. Everyone had their business, and everyone seemed to have a place to be. Eder stopped by a tanner's and studied the merchandise on sale but found himself unimpressed by the handywork. *Pa could do a better job.* He strolled from one place to another, finding himself looking into stores that sold similar to those in Croner, such as the blacksmith's and the butcher's, comparing their quality and style to that of his hometown.

Most of his time was stolen by the shops he had never seen before, like the jeweller. The man inside showed him various necklaces and earrings, each sparkling in the light with rocks of colours and shades he could never have imagined. They were presented to him with a flourish. 'For the lady of your heart, perhaps, my fine sir,' the merchant said, and Eder almost burst out laughing. No one had ever called him sir, and never had he sought a lady to give such gifts.

He walked until the insistent growling of his stomach drew his attention away from the sights of the city to the signs hanging from the buildings. He wondered where a good place would be to find a meal, and he decided that he would let his nose choose for him.

He had just caught a pleasant scent, when the clattering of hooves came racing towards him. Just in time, he stepped aside, feeling the rush of air as the horse rattled by. Eder looked on, shocked that anyone would ride so fast with so many people around. Atop the horse, long golden hair billowed from a pale skinned lady, her jerkin tight around her waist. Moments later, a second horse came rushing after it. 'Make way for the queen,' the rider shouted.

Eder shook his head. *Everyone in this city has lost their senses.* He crossed the road, approaching a building with three helmets stacked into a pyramid on its sign. Inside, the fire was crackling, freshly laid. A handful of patrons sat at tables, nibbling on morning meals and speaking between themselves.

The innkeeper watched as he approached the counter. 'How can I help you, young sir?'

Eder flushed. 'I'd like some food, please.'

He raised an eyebrow. 'You have the coin?'

He nodded, fishing the small pouch from his breast pocket. The innkeeper looked at him a moment, and then his face softened. 'Not from round here, are you?'

'No, mister. Only arrived this morning.'

The innkeeper leaned on the counter and looked down at him. 'Here's some advice for you, lad: keep your coin in your pocket until you're asked for it. Many people in this city would rob you of all you had if they saw you had it. Keep it hidden, and only show what you have once you're asked. That way they can't change their price.'

Eder nodded, uncertain at the advice. He slipped the pouch back into his pocket. 'How much do I owe for a meal?'

He smiled at him. 'This once, nothing. You'll need that coin to last you, by the looks of things. Sit at the table over there, by the fire. I'll have someone bring you some stew from last night.'

Thanking him, Eder hurried over and settled into a chair. The table was sticky, and the chair rocked, but Eder was pleased to be by the fire. He set his pack between his legs, letting the heat seep into his bones. It was a relief to be out of the wind, and he thought he could have quite happily slept where he sat.

A moment later, a woman with hair the colour of midnight placed a bowl of steaming broth on the table. A hunk of bread, lathered with fat, sat on a plate next to it. 'I'll be back with a drink,' she said, placing a spoon next to his bowl. He stared at the portion before him and turned in his chair to look at the innkeeper watching over him with a smile. He nodded to Eder as he worried at a cup, then placed it under the counter.

As Eder turned back to his meal, his elbow caught the spoon and it slipped from the table. He made to catch it, but his fingers were too slow, tumbling out of reach. Just before it clattered to the floor, the spoon stilled in the air and leapt back into his palm. Eder sat up, glanced around to check if anyone had seen, then dipped the spoon into the stew. The first bite burnt his tongue, but he only slowed only to blow across the next spoonful.

The woman returned with a tanker of mead and chuckled. 'You must be hungry. Haven't seen no one eat like that but growing lads.'

He smiled sheepishly and swallowed. 'It's delicious.'

'More like you're starving. I'll fetch you some more bread and tell Sara that a guest approves of her cooking.' She turned on her heel and strolled back to the kitchen, collecting an empty plate as she went.

'Thank you, miss,' Eder said when she returned.

'Call me Dhalia.'

He bobbed his head, popping a chunk of bread into his mouth. She pulled a seat next to him and perched by the table. 'What brings you to the city, then, boy?'

'Looking for someone to train me,' he said around a mouthful.

'Oh? In what?'

'The stables, miss. I'm going to the palace, first, though. I need to speak to King Dessius.'

Dhalia burst out in laughter before turning to the innkeeper. 'Hey, Muttrow, the lad's looking to speak to King Dessius.' A few hushed laughs came from other patrons as the innkeeper chuckled. Eder felt his cheeks burn and he avoided looking at her as she turned around. She looked at him for a moment, then her expression turned to shock. 'You *have* heard, haven't you? The king's dead. Assassinated.'

He paused, looking to her to see if she were joking. 'Well, I'm not looking for the king exactly...' he said slowly.

'Good, because unless you can speak to the dead, you're a week too late.'

The innkeeper shouted across from the counter. 'Dhalia, I don't pay you to sit and socialise with my customers. Get back to work.'

She rolled her eyes and gave Eder a wink. 'Ain't no pleasing him. You know, there's a man who's going to take me away from here. He doesn't know it yet, but he comes in some evenings. Sits right where you're sitting now, and I hide from old Muttrow. Me and this man, a palace guard, he is, we can talk and talk. He makes me laugh like no one else can. He's going to steal me away one day, just you see.' She flashed him a smile and rose from her chair. 'Take care, boy. I hope you find the person you're looking for.'

Eder nodded silently, pushing more of the stew into his mouth. *So the king's really dead. How can anyone know which rumours to listen to and which is just town gossip?* He sighed, wiping up the last of his stew with the remaining bread before sitting back and watching the flames. He studied them intently, letting his mind wander and his vision distance from his thoughts. *Grand Pa would be proud that I've made it here. Pa probably hasn't had another thought about me since I left,* he thought bitterly. Yet, could he forget his only child? There had been a time when he had treated him as his son, and Eder recalled how he would play tricks on Pa, moving tools just as he was absent-mindedly reaching for them. He would hide and jump out at him, startling him. Eder had never understood why he'd resented his abilities, and he knew he had tried to make him stop, to teach him that it was wrong. It was Grand Pa who had stopped him when his non-violent training proved ineffective. He had made sure Eder could practice in safety, but his father never looked at him the same again.

Eder blinked a few times, staring at the flames, now quelled and low. He took a breath and turned his focus away; the flames sprang back to life, roaring around the logs.

Eder checked his pack, stacked his plate and bowl, and returned them to the counter. 'Thank you, mister.'

Muttrow raised an eyebrow. 'You'll put my staff out of work doing things like that, lad. Take care, and next time I won't be quite as charitable.'

Eder ducked out of the door and joined the streams of people that ran through the streets. Jumping from one current to another, he let the tides sweep him closer to the heart of Corazin. He followed his feet, trusting his general sense of direction to take him near to where he needed to go. *So the rumours were true, for once, or at least in part. I'm sure you can't pull a man's blood from his eyeballs. I wonder if I'll find the truth when I find my tutor.*

Despite his reassurances, the thought troubled him. Maxia within the city. He had heard of hermits who had practised their art, but they had lived far into the countryside, rarely encountered, and only ever by desperate strangers. Rarely did Maxia risk living as a part of society, and if they did, none knew of what they were capable of.

Eder remembered the story a minstrel had told around the beach pyre at Verán festival some summers ago. It had been about a man who had been travelling alone, heading east through the Ferro Forest towards Tronko. He had been setting up camp one evening, the fire just beginning to crackle, when he heard the first

170

howl. He had thought nothing of it, not until the deep thunder came from the trees around his camp. Not waiting for the attack, the traveller had thrown himself to his feet and fled, clutching his walking staff and lute as he did. The wolves stayed to claim what he left, and he knew that bandits would pick at whatever they left. The pack fought over what they found, all except two. These two hounded him as he fled further and further from the path in an attempt to lose them. They nipped at his ankles, but every time they came near, they earned a crack on the head from his staff.

The minstrel had said that he had run all night, not stopping lest his respite was the moment Fate claimed him. So he ran. Even when the pounding of paws and snarling snouts of his pursuers had left him for carrion, he ran. It was only as morning light flitted through the trees that the man stumbled to his knees, exhaustion knocking him from his feet. With the road lost, and no chance of rescue, he accepted the path Fate had set for him. Lying on his back, he watched the birds, listened to the trees, making peace with the time he had been granted.

Then he caught the scent of smoke. Shocked, he scrambled to his feet and sought its source. Sure enough, he found a hut and fell down at its door, begging for someone to help him.

Beyond this, the man apparently remembered little else besides that his wounds were wrapped and his belly filled. His memory only resumed when he removed a blindfold from around his head, a rucksack on his shoulders. Before him, the road led out into the hilly landscape of Tronko. He turned around and looked about to see if he could find an answer to his renewed state, but behind him, dense forest showed no path.

Eder racked his mind, trying to recall a tale of a Maxia within a city. There were fleeting mentions of the crown's Maxia that every king kept at his side, but they were often an accessory to the triumph of the story, a mere mention as opposed to the focal point of it. For a group of them to converge and to act violently was unheard of.

He shook himself and returned his attention to his surroundings. Turning, he realised he had passed beyond the inner walls of the city. Here, the houses were larger, with greater space between them. They were less stacked, taking up more room as opposed to stretching to reach the heights of the walls. He looked down the street and saw it cut off by a wall to form a junction. This wall was comparatively short to the rest of the structures in the city and Eder though a man could easily breach it if he were to stand on another's shoulders.

Hurrying to the end of the street, Eder checked one way, then another, spying two palace guards standing before an archway that led onto the grounds.

He took a moment, straightened his clothes and ran a hand through his hair, then strode over to them purposefully. 'I am here seeking an audience with the queen. I am to meet the court Maxia.'

The two guards looked at each other. One with a bushy moustache raised an eyebrow. 'Aye, and I'm looking for a castle and a pretty thing to warm my sheets. Ain't happening, lad.'

Eder stood dumbfounded before them. 'You-you don't understand. I'm expected, you see.'

The other man chuckled. He was older, a scar across his cheekbone. 'You're expected by the Maxia, are you?' He shook his head. 'Piss off, lad. Beggars aren't allowed near the palace.'

Worth a shot, he thought grimly. Behind the guards, a man paced, his gaze distant, not seeing the world around him. He wore fine robes of colours that Eder had never seen on a man before. 'Hey, mister, please tell these guards to let me pass. I *must* see the queen.'

The nobleman looked up, startled. One of the guards growled and stepped forward. The man behind blinked a moment, as though not understanding how he came to be there, but when he looked over, amusement crossed his face. 'Can't handle a wee city rat, lads?'

The scarred man muttered something and gave Eder a shove. 'Get! Before you get us stuck with mucking the stables.' Eder let himself be pushed but stepped back towards them.

'Please, mister. I'm here to see Master Reinhick. He...' Eder faltered, wondering if admitting his intention was worth the risk. 'I'm hoping he can teach me.'

The man's eyebrows raised, and the guards flinched. One of them loosened his sword, but the man hurried forward and tapped the guard's elbow, keeping the sword sheathed. He crouched before Eder and looked him square in the eyes. 'You be careful saying things like that, boy. If it weren't for me, I fear your head and your neck would not be so well acquainted.'

'But I *must* see him. I've travelled for weeks, all the way from Croner.'

'Then you'd best keep going. I'm sorry to bring you ill news, boy, but Reinhick was killed the same night as King Dessius. King Raiden has no Maxia yet, and a new Maxia won't accept apprentices for a time, I'm sure.'

Eder's head swam and the ground tilted beneath him. 'He's... dead?'

'Yes, boy, and you'd do well to learn to listen before you learn anything else.'

'But-but who else can teach me? I can't go back. I-I've—'

The man looked at him sympathetically. 'If you want my advice, keep it to yourself. Use it as little as possible. Folk won't treat you kindly for your... talents, especially not here.' He patted Eder on the shoulder and rose. 'May your path be true and your journey clear.' He hurried back onto the grounds and out of sight, leaving Eder feeling dazed.

'Well?' the moustached guard snapped. 'What're you still doing here? Get out of my sight, before I treat you like the foul-blooded scum you are.' He drew his sword and took a step forward. Eder glanced at his foot as he made to take another step, but as he brought his boot down, it slid out from underneath him as though he had trodden on ice. Eder turned and ran, glancing over his shoulder to see the guard picking himself from the floor; the other guard had paled, hand on hilt. A shout chased him, but Eder did not linger to see if anyone pursued him too.

Chapter XIII

Eder ran through the inner city, past the walls, and shoved his way into the crowds. He spotted an alley away from the critical eyes of the street and ducked into its shade. He threw himself down against the wall and let his chest fall behind his knees. He buried his face, feeling his cheeks burn. *I can't go back. This can't be it.*

'You okay down there?' A frail voice echoed down the alley.

He looked up, glaring at whoever spoke. Without thinking, a howling gust swept down the alley, gathering up dust and coughing it out the other end of the alley. Eder heard a cry as the person was engulfed in the cloud, and a few surprised shouts came from the street. He listened, but no other sounds came his way.

'Maybe they're all right,' he mumbled to himself, sagging against the wall. 'I should just find a trade and be like everyone else.'

A presence neared him, and he rolled his eyes. 'Leave me alone,' he shouted, looking up. The alley was empty; a few confused looks peered in from the street. Eder frowned. He could still feel the presence.

He pushed himself to his feet, eyeing the shadows warily. 'Who's there?' he said, keeping the nervousness from his voice. Eder spotted a broken spoke from a wheel on the floor nearby, noting its position lest he need it.

The Heart's Whittler, a voice said, clear in his mind. It was male, rough, hissing slightly.

Eder straightened, eyes darting from side to side. 'Show yourself. I'm not afraid of you,' he said, taking a step back towards the street he had come from. The presence disappeared just as abruptly as it had come, but Eder's skin crawled. He grabbed his backpack and ran back onto the street, putting as much distance between him and the alley.

His heart raced, and a sweat coated his brow, but he still felt as though he were being watched. *Breathe,* he told himself. *I'm hearing things. The heart's whittler? Nonsense.* He ducked into a shop, ignoring the baker as he offered him a sample of his finest tarts. *I can't stay here. I need to leave. But where? There's nowhere else.* He pretended to browse a tray of sticky pastries. He touched the pouch of coin in his breast pocket and decided he might see if he could perk his spirits. He chose a small pastry braid glistening in honey. Pulling his pouch after receiving a price, he took his pastry and savoured the flavours. Moments later, he was licking the sticky sweetness from his fingers. *This city is full of bad luck,* he told himself. *Whatever I do, I'm leaving this cursed city right now.*

He hurried back through the streets, though whether he was going north or south, he knew not. One thing was for sure: he was going downhill, toward the outer wall.

A shoulder barged into him, and an arm caught his chest to stop him falling into a pair of legs, a patch on knee of the trousers catching his eye. 'Watch it,' the voice snapped, but when Eder turned to apologise, he only saw a girl marching away from him. He watched for a moment, brow furrowed as bodies turned to watch her go by.

His eyes widened, and his hand went to his pocket. Empty.

'Hey!' Eder charged after her, shouting for people to move out of the way. Angry yells chased him, but he left them to shake a fist at him. The girl broke into a sprint, not looking back. He kept his gaze on the brown hair that bobbed through the crowds, disappearing behind bodies and reappearing moments later. He was gaining on her when she ducked down a narrow side-street, and he put on a burst of pace before she could turn out of it. He was just in time to see her stroll into the next street. He barrelled into the crowd, knocking a man to the ground as he scanned the crowd for her. A flicker of brown hair turned at a crossroads and into the next street. Eder apologised quickly, crossed the road, and hurried down another alley, ignoring the offended looks behind him. The next street was quieter, but he kept his eyes trained on the junction to his left. He spied the girl, now walking, moving with a purpose, but in no apparent rush. If he had not noticed the patch on her trousers, he doubted he would have suspected the girl at all.

He kept after her, maintaining a brisk pace. She never looked back, her shoulders relaxed, though he could see her recovering her breath. She turned up one street, then down another. He was just about to reach out and grab her shoulder when she bolted, heading for a deserted alley. This one was longer than the others and Eder gave up the chase in frustration. Instead, he scanned for what might be strewn around; a length of rope bundled on cart caught his eye. As the girl ran past, the rope leapt from the cart, tangling around her feet. She hit the ground with a grunt and he jogged to catch up before standing over her, his hand out. To his surprise, he was met with a grin.

'Not bad,' she nodded, climbing to her feet. 'Not bad at all.' She tossed him the pouch of coin. 'Follow me.'

He stared at her, bewildered. 'Excuse me? Follow you?'

She paused and looked over her shoulder. 'Yeah. Not deaf, are you?'

'You *just* tried to rob me.'

She tilted her head from side to side. 'Actually, I did rob you. You just caught me.'

'Not a great pickpocket then.'

'Better than most,' she shrugged. 'You're the first to get their money back, so by anyone else's standards, I'm not a pickpocket.'

'Except you just stole from me.'

She rolled her eyes. 'Yes, but no one else knows that. You're not a criminal unless you get caught.'

'But you still committed the crime? And *I* caught you,' Eder said, struggling to believe he was having an argument with someone who had just tried to steal his coin.

'Then I've only ever committed one crime, and you're not going to tell anyone.'

'What makes you so sure?' he said, making to step the other way.

She stopped, and looked at him, frustrated that she had to explain herself. 'Firstly, no one cares if a lost street kid gets mugged. Secondly, you're going to come with me anyway, and where we're going, you don't talk about what you've done, all that matters is what you've got.'

Eder frowned. 'Why would I go with you?'

'Oh, I'm sorry, you've got somewhere else to go? Look, unless you want to sleep on the road again, you're going to come with me. Also, it looks bad if I go back with nothing. At least you're... something.' She turned on her heel and marched off, leaving the alley and Eder behind. He stood baffled for a moment, torn. She had a point: he had nowhere to go. *No harm in seeing what she's offering.* The temptation of a night in shelter proved too great.

The girl led him through a labyrinth of alleys and roads, and Eder was soon sure even she had little clue where they were for a time. He tried to make some sort of conversation, to find out who she was and where they were going, but his attempts were met with a contemptuous look as though he were more of a trailing inconvenience.

'Wait here,' she said abruptly.

Eder looked about, unsure. They were stood outside of a house on the eastern side of the city, its rafters old and many of the shutters missing. The longer he had followed her through the city, the higher his doubts built, but now, as she knocked and the door opened ajar, he was ready to run and leave this crazed city behind him.

The door opened, and she was accepted. Eder was just about to follow when it shut in his face. He scowled and nodded to himself. *Of course. No one in this bloody city has any manners.* Sitting on the step in front of the house, he watched people trundle along. Here, the people looked forlorn and tired. Their clothes were more ragged and patched, their cheeks a little more pinched. Yet, it was like everywhere else: everyone had to be somewhere. It reminded him of the beehive that Mr Tooker cared for in Croner.

He glanced to the sky, guessing it must have been after midday. His thoughts returned to Grand Pa. At this time of the day, the plants had already been watered and any ingredients for his concoctions had been picked and gathered. He was likely sat at his workbench, pipe champed between his teeth as he mixed poultices and scribbled notes. When Eder had left, he had been studying tree barks and their qualities, especially when burnt. He would assess their effects, use the ash in mixtures, feeding it to animals or spreading it on skin. His experiments were seldom fruitful, but once he had found that a certain recipe of mashed whistle root and tascus leaf created a salve that burned when applied to the skin. Eder had heard Grand Pa yelp from outside, and he had rushed to see what he had done. The old man was wiping it off of his forearm and inspecting the skin, but his eyes were bright with excitement. The salve had turned the skin a light pink, and any further experiments he had done he had done on captured animals. 'Better to test it on them, first,' he had told Eder once. 'If it's going to burn a hole through skin, better to know before I put it on a child thinking it'll heal them.'

The animals were always used to their fullest. Grand Pa never gravely harmed an animal unless he was going to kill it for its meat. On occasion, the animal would already be dead before he started his experiments, and that part of the animal was discarded and buried so as not to harm any other creature.

The door opened behind Eder, making him start and jolting him from his reverie. A boy, a season or two older, stood over him, a disgusted look on his face. 'Where'd she find you?'

Eder climbed to his feet. 'Excuse me?'

'Come on, Leis wants to meet you.' He left Eder standing dumbly, not waiting to shut the door behind him. The exterior matched the interior: dimly lit, bits and bobs strewn everywhere. Eder made his way carefully through the corridor, avoiding treading on any of the litter as he went. Two rooms sat on either side, doors missing, their contents scant. At the end, the boy stood holding another door open. Warmth emanated from the room, and inside Eder was shocked by the contrast. A fire crackled in the hearth. The floor was swept; chairs sat neatly around a table; light streamed in through shutters. Finery stood on various surfaces: gleaming candelabras, tapestries, a decanter of wine stood central on the table. A haze sat over the room, a soft, earthy smell filling it, reminding Eder of Grand Pa's experiments.

The girl who had robbed him sat at the table, her feet crossed on the surface as she glared at her fingernails, picking dirt from under them. At the hearth, a man sat with a pipe, sending clouds as white as his hair swirling to the beams overhead. He stood when Eder came in and gave him a warm smile.

'Greetings, friend. Please, take a seat.' Eder hesitated, but the other boy gave him a shove and he sat opposite the man he presumed was Leis. 'I must apologise, this is most unorthodox. We don't usually accept visitors, especially not ones who have been tangled up in business.'

'Business?' Eder exclaimed. 'The girl tried to steal from me.'

'Indeed,' the man grinned around his pipe. 'Tried. Might I ask what your name is?'

'Eder. Most people call me Ed.'

'Eder it is. Your mother gave you a name—a fine one too—it would be a waste if never used.'

'I'm sure she won't mind. Childbirth took her before I knew her.'

He raised an eyebrow. 'All the more reason to treasure your name. The only other gift she could give you was a name. For your life, she gave her own. There is no greater sacrifice than that which a mother gives. For that, I would treasure your name above all else.'

'Pa would argue otherwise,' Eder said blinking, reining his tongue under control. 'What is this place?'

'A building. Just another carcass from another's life.'

'So that makes you parasites?'

The man chuckled. 'Yes, I suppose we are.' He looked over to the girl at the table. 'Lucida, you never said he was quick-witted.'

'Quick enough to catch her,' the older boy smirked, leaning on the doorframe. He had a set jawline and shaggy hair, his eyes dark.

Leis sat forward, leaning on his knees and puffing smoke into the fire. 'You must have questions, Eder. Please, now is the time to voice them.'

Several questions leaped to mind. *What am I doing here? Are you going to kill me? What do you people do?* He took a breath, steadied his mind. 'Why was I brought here?'

'Because you have no place to go. Next question.'

'So this is an orphanage?'

'No. It is a refuge where you can hone your skills before entering a trade. Next.'

Eder bit his lip. 'What skills? Thievery, like the girl?'

'If those are your skills, then perhaps.' He met Eder's eyes. 'After staying here, some my guests have become part of the council, some have become smiths and traders, others have become bandits and killers. I have hosted those with pure hearts, and those who believe Fate has dealt them a path through brambles and ivy. I do not dictate what you become, only that you become the best you can be. For example, Lucida here is a pickpocket like this city has never seen before. Never caught—well, not until today, that is. Oskar is blessed with the ability persuade anyone to his cause. Rhetoric is his art, and with us, he hones it, collecting his secrets and sharing them for profit.'

A glimmer of pride shone in the boy's eye, but Eder ignored it. Instead, he frowned. 'And what do you profit from this?'

'Very good, Eder. You're a thinker.' He puffed several times, aligning his words. 'Everyone who stays here must bring what they earn from the day. It is shared between us. We are a community. When no one else will help us, we must help ourselves.'

'So what does that make me? Some sort of prize?'

'That depends on what you bring,' he said. Eder gripped his backpack tighter.

'Don't the guards know what you're doing here? You'll be stormed the moment you're found out.'

He nodded. 'That's how it ought to be, but the guards are blind. The slip of a coin into the right hands and life continues as normal.'

Eder stared into the flames, surprised at the revelation. How could the guard not protect the people? To not throw these thieves in prison was surely as criminal as those they left. 'I'm sorry, but I have nothing to offer you. I came here searching for a future, for an honest tutor, but it appears both are dead.'

A knowing look spread across Leis' face and Lucida shifted at the table, swinging her feet from the table. 'Welcome to the real world,' the man said. 'You're not from around here, and I'd bargain you've a long way to go yet. Stay a night. Rest.' It was no question.

Eder narrowed his eyes. 'I've spent enough nights finding shelter beyond the walls. Tonight will be no different.'

'Perhaps, but when you have a pocket of coin, and a backpack of fine craft, one shouldn't be surprised if he wakes to find himself at the mercy of a blade.' The old man held his gaze. Eder could tell his words were already plotted, and his next move had already been countered in the man's mind.

Eder started assessing the room. The old man would be of no trouble. He could break the chair leg and leave him struggling. The girl would be upon him quickly, but he saw no weapon on her and Eder reckoned he could out-strength her. Oskar would be difficult. He was a head or so taller than Eder, with broad shoulders and thick arms; he didn't fancy his chances in a brawl, but hot ashes might buy him enough time to escape.

'I'll make you a deal, Eder.' The voice pulled him from his thoughts as Leis watched him carefully. 'You stay here for the night, take refuge with us, and you can see what it is we do. Lucida and Oskar will take you with them, show you a trick or two.'

'But Leis,' Lucida started. 'That's not fair, he'll only get in the—'

'Enough,' he barked, silencing her. 'You brought him here, you will be responsible for him. It'll be good for you.'

'You know I only work alone,' she muttered.

'If you're as good as you boast you are, you'll have no trouble.'

Eder eyed them warily. 'What if I do? What happens if I stay one night?'

'If you stay with us a night, you may leave tomorrow, whenever you wish. A free man once more. You have already spent valuable time with us, and this time must be accounted for. Pay your debt, Eder, then you shall be free.'

He looked between them, trapped in a den of wolves. *What choice do I have?* 'Fine.'

Lucida tutted and stood, pushing past Oskar, but he followed her. The man watched them go. 'I'll talk to them shortly, but for now it seems we have some privacy.' Leis set his pipe aside and knitted his hands on his lap. 'I know this seems daunting, and I don't expect you to trust us—not yet. After the first night, no one is ever asked to stay. All of them are guests, welcome as long as they pay their share. Some step out of the door and I never see them again, others come back after some years, a changed person, but thankful for their time here.'

'What about them?' he nodded to the door. 'How long have they been "guests?"'

Leis pondered a moment, as if weighing how much to tell him. 'They were the first. I've known them all their lives. They were dropped at my door one night, though who delivered them, I don't know. I reckon they were meant for another door, but Fate has its way, like it or not. Whether or not they are siblings by blood, I've raised them as such, and they protect each other as such.'

'So, there are others?'

Leis stood, moving slowly as he did. It was only now that Eder noticed the vibrancy of his robes and the way they silently shifted over one another. 'At the moment there are four, not including yourself. You'll meet the others this evening.' He poured wine into two goblets, both of a fine metal and decorated with colour and fine etching. Sipping at his own, Leis held the other to Eder. 'What skills have you, Eder? Where might you benefit us?'

He frowned, tasting the wine. 'I'm not sure. I have very little talent. My father never taught me his trade, and I have nothing remarkable to say of myself.'

'And yet, you caught Lucida. That is no small feat.'

'Luck,' he dismissed.

'A talent in itself.' Leis studied him and hummed. 'Well, you have two eyes. You can keep a look out and watch the others at their work. Perhaps quick learning will be your talent,' he suggested. 'Please, excuse me, Eder. I must speak to the siblings. Once they are ready, you'll leave with them. I have my own business to attend to this evening.'

Chapter XIV

Lucida dragged him past a group of people then climbed onto a statue. They were in the middle of a populated square, people jostling simply to get by. The volume here seemed to have doubled in comparison to along the streets, and Eder wondered if this was really a preferable time to leave your home if it meant battling through this.

A hand pulled him up to sit beside her, but her eyes were elsewhere. Somewhere in the foray, Oskar moved. Her gaze trained on him, she never took her sight from him for a moment. Despite his efforts, Oskar proved as elusive to Eder as a spooked octopus.

'What are we doing? I thought you were supposed to be showing me what you do?'

'Watching. This *is* what we do.'

'Watching doesn't steal valuables from people.'

She resisted an eye roll, tutting instead. 'Look, you want to learn? Shut your mouth and I'll teach when I'm ready to teach.'

Eder frowned at her but did as asked. He surveyed the crowds, trying to see what she did. There was something about the people here, but it took Eder a moment to understand what.

After dragging him through the streets, taking convoluted journeys through alleys as opposed to simply following the roads, Eder had realised that, despite the density, they were all very different. Many in the outer ring walked with a limp or vacant stare, their hands scarred and calloused, clothes stained and dirtied. The closer to the palace, the fewer these people became. Folk walked instead with a purpose, an energy that the others had seemed to lack. They had colour in their cheeks and pattern to their clothes. Whilst many of these people worked just as hard, they were, Eder guessed, better trained and more skilled. Even looking at the shop fronts around him, the rafters were painted, shutters had locks, and the wares on display were finer, better crafted, much like the people they attracted.

They were not quite beyond the inner wall, but it loomed high enough that they were close; it must have been the closest the residences came to crossing the wall's boarder. Eder noticed another difference: the people seemed more pleasant. There were fewer grumbled comments and snapped phrases. There were less glares and suggestions of violence. Instead of fists and blades, the wars here were fought behind fake smiles and turned backs.

'Alright, Eddie,' Lucida said, turning to him. 'Why are we here?'

Eder looked at her, baffled for a moment. 'So you can teach me....'

She looked to the sky for a moment and sighed. 'Yes, but why *here.*'

His cheeks flushed. 'Because of the people here. They're richer. They've got money.'

She hummed, tilting her head in part agreement. 'Yes, the purses here tend to be heavier than further out, but that's not all. Look again.'

He turned back to the crowd and he scanned individuals, looking to see if one of them might hold an answer. He shrugged.

'Because there's so many people,' she said, already exasperated. 'Think about it, Eddie. If I had bumped into you here, would you have noticed?'

'I'd hardly call it a bump but….'

She saw the realisation on his face. 'Exactly. With this many people, you can't help jostling into somebody. You're always brushing past someone, knocking into another, so you ignore it. There is no greater gift in our profession than ignorance. It gives you the opportunity to be less delicate when your hand's in someone's pocket.'

Eder grinned, admiring the logic.

'It's all part of something called sleight of hand,' Lucida continued. 'At its core, it's essentially the art of distraction and deception. Send someone's attention elsewhere when it would be better paid to their pockets. Like I did with you, earlier. I distracted you long enough to pull your purse.' She returned her gaze back to the crowd, searching again for Oskar. She found him quickly, and Eder still failed. 'That's the first lesson. Next, you select your target. Who do you pick?'

Eddie floundered, again hoping an example from the crowd would inspire him. 'Someone who looks wealthy?'

She smiled. 'Nice try. In reality, you can get just as much money by the outer walls as you can here, it would just take a few more opportunities. However, the more you strike the higher the risk of getting caught. Look for someone who is going to be easy, who is as risk-free as possible. Someone practically asking you to take their money.'

'I was asking you to rob me?' he said dubiously.

She threw him a look. 'You were painfully obvious. You're not from around here, you don't know where you are, and you didn't know where you were going. Strangers in a strange city are less likely to act out than locals.'

He stared at her. 'How could you possibly know that?'

She shrugged nonchalantly, obviously enjoying having knowledge over him. 'It was in the way you walked—I guess you could call it experience. Now stop licking your wounds and pay attention. Whilst we've been talking, Oskar has been in the crowd, looking for a target. Once he's found someone, he'll signal to me. That's when the distraction begins, and that's when I'll move. He'll keep the target busy while I go in, take what there is to take, and stroll on by. The target doesn't even know what's happened until he walks away.'

Eder could not keep the smile from his face. 'Leis said Oskar was the best at persuading people.'

'He is,' she said proudly. 'There are two ways to go about what we do. Straight to the point, or… well, *his* way.' She shook her head. 'He calls it an art. He takes from right under their noses, then convinces them that he's helping them. I've seen him do it a million times. He befriends them, pulls them onto his side. He'll shake their hand or jostle them, and that's that, the money is as good as his. Once he even convinced the target not to chase after me, to let him go instead.'

Eder raised his eyebrow. 'Not your style then?'

She shook her head, then sat up abruptly. 'That's the signal.' Eder looked about, oblivious. Lucida dropped a hand under the hem of her shirt and retrieved a small pouch of coin, dropping it onto his lap. 'That's your lesson over. Watch carefully, then follow Oskar after a couple of minutes.'

'Where did this come from?' he asked as she jumped down.

She looked back over her shoulder. 'Pulled it as we got here. In case you're not successful,' she winked. 'Can't have my first pupil going back with nothing.'

He shook his head, struggling to recall an opportunity that she could have taken it.

Tucking the pouch away, he watched as her chestnut hair weaved its way through the crowd. For a second, he searched for Oskar, but when he returned his attention back to where Lucida had been, she was gone. He sat up, alarmed, only to see her reappear several paces to the side. Ahead of her, Eder spotted Oskar. He was engaged in conversation with an older man who wore a bright tunic. The two were laughing, Oskar patting the man on the shoulder.

Suddenly, Oskar lurched forward as though he had been shoved. Oskar barged into the orange-dressed man, then whirled, furiously grabbing a member of the crowd by the shoulder and spinning them to face him. The man looked alarmed and quickly lifted his hands in defence while the man in the colourful tunic was at Oskar's side, seemingly berating the man too. Eder blinked, surprised at the sudden turn of events. He searched for Lucida, but guessed the accident had thrown them off, attracting too much attention to the scene to make a move.

Eder watched as Oskar and his companion continued to harass the man who had pushed Oskar. He was evidently distressed, and he held his hand out to Oskar, offering him something. Oskar nodded, taking it, then the man hurried away, not looking back. Oskar and the other man continued to talk for a moment, shaking their heads and laughing, the anger dissipating out of them. They shook hands, nodded a few times, and Eder understood their farewells. He watched another moment as Oskar stepped through the crowds, slipping between people before heading for an opening into a street. Eder jumped down from the statue and made for the same direction.

As he was jostled and pushed, he kept his wits about him, searching for opportunities that the others might have looked for. He was surprised at how little attention people paid to him, and although he was tall for his age, he was still smaller than many of the people in the square. They elbowed past, ignoring him as though he were no more than a wall to walk around as opposed to someone trying to go somewhere.

He finally broke free of the crowd and trotted up the street, heading along the road as he searched for the siblings. Just when he was beginning to wonder if they had left him, a shout came from a side street. 'Eddie, over here,' Lucida waved. He hurried over, relieved to be away from the rabble and odours of the square. 'So,' she said, leaning against a building. 'What'd you see?'

Eder looked between them, confused. 'Well, Oskar was talking to someone when he got shoved into. It caused too much of a scene, so you got out of there, not risking acting with so many eyes on you.'

'Oh, really?' Her eye twinkled and she held her palm out. 'So how do you explain this?' A leather pouch sat on her hand, clinking as she bounced it in her palm. Oskar swiped it away.

'Try not to make it too obvious,' he hissed, glaring at her.

Eder stared at them, his jaw slack. 'How did you get it?'

'It's as I said,' Lucida laughed. 'It's all about distraction.'

Even Oskar had a smirk to his face. 'No one pushed me. It was part of the distraction. Luce knew when to act, and after, I even managed to get compensation for being "sorely inconvenienced."' He flourished a coin along his fingers, before slipping it to his pockets.

'They *gave* you their money?'

'Didn't even have to ask.'

Eder shook his head. 'Amazing.'

Lucida pushed herself off the wall. 'Now it's your turn.' She gave him a nudge back towards the crowd.

Looking back at her, he felt a flutter of uncertainty. 'You're not coming too?'

Oskar shook his head. 'Never return to the scene of the crime. Well, not for a few hours anyway.'

Lucia nodded, urging him away. 'Go on. Unless you're scared that you can't do it.' Her eyes sparkled with mischief and Eder's cheeks burned. 'We'll be here when you get back. Remember, running makes you guilty before you're even accused. Oh, and if I didn't mention it earlier, try not to get caught.'

'Right,' he said, still hoping one of them would accompany him. When neither made to move, he took a breath and turned, heading back to the square. 'Find a target,' he muttered to himself, 'distract them, then move.'

Joining the crowd, he wondered what his style would be. He thought he would be much better at Lucida's approach; he didn't have the confidence to confront someone and befriend them whilst their money was in his pocket. It seemed far easier to get what you wanted and leave.

He slipped into the crowd, becoming one with its motions. The noise of the people became overwhelming and Eder focussed on the task at hand. He continued to be jostled about and he made a complete loop of the statue before realising he would never find anyone this way. Instead, he forced his way out to the shopfronts that encapsulated the square. He pressed himself against a wall, took a breath, and surveyed the faces that shuffled past. It dawned on him that he had no idea who had money and who walked empty-handed. Did he dare follow someone with an armful of purchases, only to discover all their coin spent?

He sighed, slumping against the wall, when he heard coins clinking. He perked up, trying to look without seeming obvious. From a nearby shop window, a vendor handed over a brimmed hat. The customer was hurriedly slipping a pouch into his jerkin pocket, eager to receive his purchase. *That'll do,* Eder thought. He let the man walk for a few paces before tailing him. An urgency suddenly came upon him. *What if he leaves straight away?*

Ducking past someone, he tried to close the distance between them. To his fortune, the man met a lady, perhaps his sister or a companion, to whom he proudly showed off his new attire. Eder stepped closer, suddenly aware of all the people pressing in around him. *It's to my advantage,* he reminded himself. He slowed as he neared and made sure to keep his arms close, but he could not help but stare at the pocket. It was deep, and although the jerkin hung at his hips, Eder was sure sneaking a hand inside without alerting the man was impossible.

Eder nearly clapped himself across the head. *What if I don't have to?* He stepped nearer until his shoulder was brushing the man's upper arm. For a moment, he was glad to be pressed in by people around him, stunting any movement. He took a breath, held his hand just above the pocket, and focussed on its contents. He forced himself to move slowly, to blot out all surrounding sounds and the people nudging him. There was a movement from the pocket, as something slowly rose to its brim. Eder watched eagerly, forcing himself to Will it slowly. Then the pouch was free, hovering above the pocket. He was just about to snatch the pouch out of the air when someone shoved into him.

His hand swiped at air as he scrambled forward, tumbling into the target. The pouch of coin hit the floor, and Eder scooped it up, clambering from his knees. The man glowered at him. 'Sorry,' Eder mumbled. 'Clumsy feet.' Eder waved as the man tutted, turning back to the conversation with his friend. Eder pocketed the pouch, heart racing. Energy filled him and he wanted to run. He wanted to climb to the roofs and skip from ledge to ledge. Instead, he forced himself to shuffle along with everyone else, though he felt all too aware of his movements, as though his walk would give him away as a thief. He even forced himself to stop and peruse a shop front before returning to the masses, then breaking down the street, and away from the bustling square. He breathed a sigh of relief, a wide grin on his face as he felt the weight in his pocket. Checking over his shoulder, he made sure he was not followed, then made his way to the road where he had left the siblings. They were sat against a wall, but stood when they saw him. Oskar was the first to speak. 'Took your time. Thought you'd been caught.'

'What a shame that would've been,' Lucida said, nudging her brother. 'So how'd you do, Eddie?'

Eder fished the pouch from his pocket with a smile, letting it hang from his finger by its drawstrings. They looked at him, stunned.

'How'd you get that?' Oskar said.

Eder shrugged. 'Guess I learned a thing or two.' He tossed the pouch to Lucida. 'For your advice, and for wasting your time this morning.'

She shook her head, weighing it in her hand. 'Not bad, Eddie. Not bad at all. So, how'd you do it?'

He looked at her, bluffing insult. 'You don't talk about what you've done, all that matters is what you've got.'

A grin broke across her face and she shared a look with Oskar. 'Yeah, you'll do, Eddie. Come on, we've got work to do.'

Chapter XV

The siblings guided him through the network of streets. Their knowledge of the roads and shortcuts staggered him as he found himself increasingly disorientated. Eder tailed them, making an effort to hear their conversation, but they neglected to open it up to him. It seemed to Eder that he was a presence when they wanted him to be, but they did not, he became little more than a shadow. Once, Lucida had dropped back to talk to him about the square and said that she wanted to compete with him to see who could get the most in an hour. Shortly after, she had become engrossed in a conversation with Oskar, eventually excluding him. Eder slunk back and followed them from a distance, turning his attention back to the people that wandered the afternoon streets. Carts rumbled by and tired drivers ushered the animals pulling them, eager to be free of the city and to an inn before nightfall.

Even after spending the hours he had there, the differences between Croner and Corazin were astounding. The people, the sprawling, stacked houses, the way of life here. Eder had never seen such affluence, but then a few minutes' walk away, he had never seen such poverty. Pa's words echoed in his mind: 'A man who flaunts his wealth has little else about him; they are less worth talking to than sheep.'

The thoughts of his family troubled him. *What would they think of me? Pa would have his strap of leather across my legs before I could finish, and Grand Pa...* shame coloured his cheeks and he looked down. The pair ahead of him laughed at something, and he glowered at them, then chastised himself. *I'm doing what I have to do to keep myself alive. They're helping me, and there's no shame in survival.* He set his shoulders, lifted his chin, and froze.

A sign caught his attention, swinging in the wind. Eder felt his mouth dry and he swayed. *It can't be.... It was nonsense.* Ahead, a shop front adorned chains of herbs and a rabbit's foot. It was a narrow building with discreet colours and shuttered windows. If he had not seen the name, he doubted he would have noticed it.

The Heart's Whittler.

Without another thought, he stepped towards it, but hesitated at the door, hand hovering over the handle. Was it a good idea to go to places whose names mysteriously appeared in his mind?

The door swung open, startling him, and a tall, broad man bundled past him, muttering an apology. Eder stared after him, opening his mouth to snap a remark, then he saw the sword hanging from his hip. Although he did not wear any guard's clothing, the sword was identical to those he had met by the palace, and that had been enough of a meeting for a lifetime.

Eder dismissed the man and caught the door before it could close. He stepped inside, careful to keep his footing quiet. The shop was gloomy. Tables and shelves presented animals and figures, all frozen in a pose, each delicately carved from different types of wood. It smelled musty, of wood shavings and wax; the scent calmed him. Nothing stirred aside from the sawdust that swirled with each step. He browsed the shelves, admiring the craft of the objects around him, smiling. *This is something I would like to do. To draw life out of a husk of wood, to take something one might toss onto a fire and then nurture it, cutting it into something worth treasuring.*

One carving caught him. Unlike the others, this was no animal, but instead a tree, carved from a pale, white wood. It was no taller than his palm, but elegantly carved, the bark etched and branches thin. With a delicate touch, he brushed the branches, admiring their sturdiness. The irony of it was not lost on him, and he wondered why someone would go to the effort of it, especially considering the quality of craftmanship of the items around it.

He lifted it, weighing it in his hand, amazed at the weight of it. He returned it to its place and made his way around the store until he found himself at the counter. Behind it, a door stood shut, and Eder surmised that the owner was somewhere beyond. On the counter, a carving of an albino crocodile sat, jaws frozen open, its tail snaked behind it.

Eder leaned closer. Of all the items, this was the finest. The entire piece was just longer than his hand, each scale was meticulously etched, its spine made of delicate, defined ridges. Yet, what he marvelled at most was not the attention to detail of the piece, but its imperfections, the consideration of a life for the creature. Its tail was shorter than it ought to have been; it had an odd count of teeth, and a scar crossed its shoulder blade.

Eder stared in awe, yet wondered who would purchase an item that appeared imperfect. Would many appreciate the character of the item? He traced his finger down its spine, admiring the wood. It was soft, as though made of soft leather. Heat seemed to emanate from it. Drawing a fingertip across its top line of teeth, he wondered how long it had taken to create something of such detail.

The jaws snapped shut and he leapt back with a yelp, wobbling the carvings behind him; a couple toppled.

You're lucky I didn't take your finger, Novo Maxia, a rough, hissing voice said.

Ed stared at the crocodile. 'Who-who speaks? Show yourself.'

The crocodile shifted, curling around itself. *Speak with your mind, lest you wish to pay for the wares you have broken.*

'What illusion is this?' he said, glancing around, sure this was some trick.

The crocodile regarded him. *A Maxia who does not know the basics of his magic. Fascinating.... Tell me, Novo Maxia, what took you so long?*

Eder stared at the crocodile, collecting himself. *You-you can hear me?*

And no one else can.

What are you? Who has cast this enchantment?

Enchantment? it scoffed. *Don't insult me so, child, otherwise I will take more than a finger from you.*

Then... what are you?

A single eye watched him from the counter. *I am what you see. My kind favour isolation from your kind. Too noisy. Too entitled. Too willing to destroy when peace will reward the same and more.*

I recognise your voice. Eder narrowed his eyes at it. *You spoke to me in the alley?*

And you took your time seeking me, Novo Maxia.

He frowned. *Why do you keep calling me that?*

The crocodile flexed a clawed foot, its tail twitching. *You are Maxia. Would you rather I call you Eder?*

Tripping on the thought, Eder wondered how it knew his name, how it knew of his abilities.

You leave your thoughts open, Novo Maxia. Anyone could peer in and see. That is, only if you are lucky. There are those who would do worse than simply pry.

I don't understand.

All the better you learn swiftly, then.

He tutted. *You speak in riddles.*

Eder sensed amusement from the creature. *If I were to speak in riddles, I fear you would understand even less, but perhaps I am wrong. Let us try. A path all must walk, yet none walk the same. All move together, crossing, entwining, yet never touching. Novo Maxia, you stand at the end of each; yours is made with each step, its direction unknown, yet once made, all others will follow.*

Eder stared at the creature blankly and the crocodile's amusement only swelled.

Speak plainly, Eder demanded. *Why summon me? Surely not just to ridicule me.*

It closed its eyes, but the presence in his mind remained steady. *Why are you here, Novo Maxia?*

I'm just going to leave, he said impatiently.

Its voice caught him, urgent. *I did not summon you from Croner. Why did you come to the Heart?*

To Corazin? To seek a teacher.

And rightly so. The creature seemed to glow, a spectre in the gloom. Eder glanced around uncomfortably, half sure he was still at the end of some prank. *You know not how to control your mind, yet you manipulate the world around you without care. Tuition is needed, Novo Maxia. Control.*

But the tutor I sought is dead. Killed with the king.

And so you give up? There is more than one tutor in this land. One stands beyond the walls as we speak.

Eder straightened. *You mean....*

Should you wish to learn, you must seek your master.

Why? Why do you tell me this?

207

The Kaminjo tree drew you. That is of no coincidence. And because of what I have already told you.

Eder looked over his shoulder. *The carving? I looked at it because it's different, not because it drew me to it.*

Did it not? Seek your master, Novo Maxia. Learn what you must, and may you lead our paths to better tidings.

The door behind the counter opened and a man looked up, startled. 'Oh! My apologies, I thought you had left.' He glanced to the crocodile, a hint of annoyance in the look as he dusted down his apron. He had brown hair, flitted with grey. It was unkempt and tangled back into a tail. 'How might I be of assistance?'

Eder looked from the crocodile to the man, the presence now disappeared from his mind. 'I-I was only looking.'

The craftsman looked at the crocodile, and his eyes widened. 'He spoke to you?'

Eder blinked, ready to flee.

'He rarely speaks to anyone.'

Eder watched him carefully. 'He said—'

'No, no. What he said was for you and you alone to hear. If he did not wish me to hear, it was for his own reasons.'

Eder looked at the crocodile, now still as the statues that sat upon the tables around him 'Why is he here?'

The carpenter raised an eyebrow, looking at the crocodile with a hint of affection. 'He's my companion, and he stays for as long as he wishes, though I must confess, he is quite good company. Normally he alerts me when someone enters, but I suppose today he felt indifferent about our relationship.' He cocked his head as he looked at the creature, as though trying to puzzle out his reasons.

Eder frowned. 'But you can speak to him. Does that not mean...?'

The man raised a bushy eyebrow, the wrinkles on his forehead multiplying. 'Any can speak to him if my companion wishes it. If not, you'll find his mind as impenetrable as the Ferro Forest.'

Eder glanced to the crocodile but found it had moved no more than when it had spoken to him. 'Well, I thank you for your time, wood smith.'

'No, no, thank you. It is not often I meet those he chooses to speak to. It leaves me with quite the riddle, trying to understand who he does and doesn't speak to. May your path be clear, friend.'

Eder hurried free of the gloom, stepping back into the street and drawing in a breath of clear air, letting it sweep clarity into his muzzy mind. He slipped further down the street, suddenly keen to be away from the shop, before leaning against a wall. He shut his eyes and lifted his face to the afternoon sun. Despite the wind, the warmth was pleasant.

'Got you, thief.' A deep voice growled as a hand clapped his shoulder.

Eder's eyes shot open. He clamped the hand to his shoulder, Willing it not to move. He was about to shove the person and make his getaway when he saw who it was. Lucida stared at him, alarm and fear on her face as she tried to pull her arm back. He relaxed his focus and she went stumbling back, as though she had been pulling a door handle with all her might and her hand had slipped. She scrambled back as he approached, offering his hand to pull her up.

Oskar was between them before he could take another step. 'What's going on?'

People were stopping to look as Lucida climbed to her feet, eyeing him like a wounded animal. Oskar drew himself to his full height over him. Behind, a man carrying two cages of chickens paused to see what would arise.

'Nothing,' Eder dismissed. 'She made me jump, that's all.' He kept his gaze on Lucida, begging her to keep quiet.

Oskar narrowed his eyes. 'That's not what it looked like to me.'

'I saw him do it, mister,' a man behind said, and others were joining him to watch. 'Shoved her hard as he could, he did.'

Eder shot him a look. The man had not been there several moments before. 'Listen, Oskar, I can explain, but…' he looked around warily. 'Not here.'

Lucida was at his shoulder. 'He's-he's—'

'Just another city rat,' Oskar spat.

'Dash his skull,' came a shout from the growing circle. Eder felt the cold stone against his back.

Oskar rolled his shoulders. 'Come on then, Eddie. See if those straight teeth of yours look any better after I'm done.'

Lucida grabbed at him, pulling him back. 'No, Oskar, he's—'

'I can explain,' Eder said, but it was apparent that Oskar was not in the mood for listening. Eder groaned inwardly. 'Meet me back at Leis's place,' he said under his breath. He flicked his gaze to the cage of chickens that had been set down. They were flitting about restlessly. He Willed the bolt to slide across from the door and it burst open, freeing the birds as they squawked and flapped into the crowd. It distracted the gathering, but Oskar moved to grab him as he tried to duck out of the way. Oskar grabbed his arm, and Eder spun, Willing him back. Oskar stumbled as though he had been shoved, losing his grip on Eder as the boy elbowed his way through the crowd.

Out in the open, he sprinted down the street. Unsure of where he was, all he knew was that he had to get out of sight. Shouts harried him, and he was certain Oskar would not be far behind.

He ducked down the next alley he saw. Dashing past a stack of crates, he turned, and Willed them to clattering across the alley, creating a low barricade. The effort drained him and he blinked to steady his vision. His heart thudded in his chest as though he had been running for several minutes, but he pushed himself on. He tried to recall what Lucida had said earlier, and what he had seen her do when she was making her get away that morning. *Running makes you guilty before you're even accused.*

Once in the next street, he slowed to a jog, made for a junction, then came to walk, becoming one with the streams of people along the street. He took the opportunity to slow his breathing, reminding himself that he would need some sort of food soon.

Where am I? He took in his surroundings as best he could, but he could only determine that he was near the outer wall. None of the buildings were familiar, but then they all looked the same to Eder. He searched the signs of shops and inns, not finding any he recognised. In the distance, he could see the mountain beyond the walls. *The mountains are north. If the palace is between me and it, I must be south somewhere, probably more east.*

One sign looked familiar: three helmets stacked upon one another. *I'm back to where I was this morning,* he realised.

His brow furrowed as he walked back along the streets, trying to retrace his steps and passing the bakery he had visited. He longed to go back and find another honeyed braid, but he knew his coin was better saved. From there, he recognised where he had first met Lucida.

Navigating his way back through the alleys proved more difficult, and he found himself doubling back to make sure he was on the right trail. All the while, he glanced over his shoulder, sure he would see Oskar charging towards him. It was only as Eder spied the rope hanging from the cart that he knew he had been successful in retracing his steps.

The way to Leis' was less clear in his mind. He trusted his feet to take him where he had to go, but the longer he walked, the surer he was that he would never find it again.

The sun was casting an orange hue across the sky when he recognised, by chance, the run-down front of the house further down the street. As he stepped up to the door, his stomach twisted in knots as he approached, but he knocked, nonetheless.

When the door opened, a young man with a thin nose and angular jaw answered. He looked at Eder expectantly. Eder blinked. 'Is this where Leis lives?'

The man looked him up and down. 'So, you're the new recruit.' He poked his head further out the door, frowning. 'Where's Luce and Oskar?'

'They're not back yet?' Eder said, surprised.

'No…' he looked at Eder again, but shrugged and stepped back to admit him. 'Leis is in the kitchen.'

Eder left him to shut the door and hurried down the corridor. When he stepped into the kitchen, Leis looked up from his place at the fire and smiled. 'Ah, Eder, you're back. I was wondering about you. Tell me, how did your day go?'

Eder swallowed. There was another girl in the kitchen, crushing some herbs into a slab of meat. She gave him a stiff nod but returned to her task. The other man joined her as Eder approached Leis. 'It was… educational.'

'I'm pleased you learned something,' he said, seeming content. 'And the others?'

Eder just opened his mouth as the front door banged open. Oskar's voice came from the hallway. 'Where is he? If he's come back here, I'll—' he stopped in the doorway and locked his eyes onto Eder, advancing on him. Leis was on his feet and between them, but Eder did not fancy the man to stop him. Lucida was behind him, but when she saw Eder, she flinched, colour draining from her face.

'What's going on here?' Leis' voice cut through the confusion.

Oskar stopped just in front of Leis, pointing an accusing finger over his shoulder. 'He attacked Luce. Don't know what he did, but I've never seen her scared of someone like this. He can't stay.'

Leis looked to Eder, then Lucida, who had taken shelter under the other girl's arm. 'Is this true?'

Lucida opened her mouth, but Oskar cut her off. 'I saw him do it. Put Luce on the ground. I was about to put him in his place before he ran off.'

'I can explain,' Eder stammered, trying to be heard.

Leis cut Oskar off with a raised hand. 'Then please, Eder, explain.'

He collected himself a moment, shuffling further away from Oskar as he glowered at him. 'I'd been distracted. I thought I saw a good target, but when I looked back, those two had disappeared. I thought I'd catch them up with something to show for myself.'

'And?' Leis said. 'Did you?'

Eder shook his head. 'The target was suspicious before I even got close. Shouted for the guard, but I'd ran already.'

Leis' look darkened. 'This isn't explaining your actions.'

Lucida spoke, watching Eder from across the room. 'I went up to him and pretended to be a guard. As a joke. I hadn't realised what'd happened.'

'So you pushed her away and you were going to run?' Leis finished and Eder nodded. 'That doesn't explain why Lucida hasn't taken her eyes off you, looking at you like you're a rabid dog.'

He stared at her, begging her not to say anything. She watched him carefully, biting her lip. 'I didn't want to say unless I was sure,' she said slowly. 'To accuse you of... this. But, Ed, I have to know.'

All eyes turned on him. The fire crackled, spitting sparks at the silence.

He sighed, knowing there was no way out without revealing himself. *Might as well come from my own mouth.* He looked to the ground, avoiding her reaction. 'It's true.'

Oskar glared at him. 'What's true? What are you two on about?'

Lucida's face paled, but she stepped away from the girl, coming closer. 'Oskar, when he shoved past you, Eddie never touched you. Everyone else was too distracted by the chickens, but... I saw. You just... flew backwards.'

Leis' eyes widened, and he looked more closely at Eder.

'And when I grabbed you,' she continued, 'you stopped my hand moving. It was like my arm was clamped in a vice. That was you, wasn't it?'

Eder bowed his head, the shame not false.

Oskar stepped back, his face paler. 'Magic?' he whispered.

Eder sighed. 'Yes. I'm sorry. I hadn't intended to use it, it was just a reaction, to save my own skin. Please, I'll go if you won't have me, but I promise you no harm.'

Leis said nothing but only looked at him.

'Are you kidding?' Lucida stepped closer, the fire reflecting in her eyes.

Eder looked to the chair, ready to flip it and make for the door.

'A Maxia. Working with us? We'd be unstoppable. We'd never have to struggle again.'

Oskar turned to her. 'No way. Magic was used to kill the king—you heard what they did. Stilled the air in the king's lungs and left him to choke. There's a reason it's forbidden.'

'And what we do is legal?' Lucida countered.

'It's twisted, and any who use it are filth.' Oksar glared at Eder. 'I say we hand him over to the guard. Let them deal with him.'

The girl who had been at the counter shook her head. 'According to everyone in this city, we're all filth. If he wants to go, let him, but he goes of his own will. We'd be casting out one of our own.'

'So he can just manipulate us?' Oskar said aghast. 'He could send us up in flames with the twitch of a finger. He's best put down, like the rat he is.'

Lucida tutted and looked at him as though seeing him anew. 'If he wanted us up in flames, we'd be ash already.'

Leis shifted, lowering himself back into his seat. He leaned forward, staring into the fire. 'Kaia is right. He's one of our own.' He chuckled and shook his head. 'Unremarkable, indeed, Eder.'

'Leis,' Oskar appealed. 'He uses *magic*. If he was found out he'd be hanged, and so would we.'

'Would that not be the same if anyone else were caught?'

'The guards wouldn't take a bribe on this.' Oskar's mouth was a thin line. 'You've always said never to take unnecessary risks. If he isn't one, then what is?'

Leaning back, Leis pressed his fingertips together. 'Eder is an asset. No harm has come from his presence. He stays.'

Oskar looked between each of them, hoping for an ally. His gaze lingered on Lucida but she avoided looking at him. He stormed out, slamming the door behind him.

Lucida came up to Eder. 'He'll be alright. Come on, you're safe with us.'

Leis nodded, but when he spoke, it was as though his thoughts were elsewhere. 'Get him some food. He's going to be hungry.'

Eder glanced at him, unsure if he spoke from knowledge or just as a host. The older girl, Kaia, pulled a seat out from under the table, finding a husk of bread. 'I'll have the stew ready soon.' The man, the one who had let Eder in, excused himself, saying he was going to find Oskar. Leis only nodded, staring into the fire.

Chapter XVI

They had just finished their meal and were sat around the table, a candle burning at the centre. Leis had left, to ponder and plot, Eder had been told. Hirst, the man with the thin nose, had returned without Oskar, claiming he had been eluded. Eder had learned Hirst was a locksmith by trade, but by night, he occasionally returned to the life that had raised him, using his skills to help if asked. Kaia was a serving girl, waiting on one of the nobles in the city. It was through her that Leis and his cohort learned of the secrets and gossip that brewed in the city.

'So, what can you do?' Lucida's eyes shone.

'What do you mean?' Eder said, wiping his mouth.

'Well, can you summon fire from your fingertips? Or can you make the ground shake as though near a volcano?' The others at the table leaned in, curious as to the answers, too. Eder had insisted they told him about themselves, and he told them some of who he was in a hope that he knew them as companions before they knew him as anything further. Now they knew a little more of each other, he looked between them, mischief in his eye.

'To cast fire out of thin air would demand an exhausting amount of energy,' he confessed.

Kaia frowned. 'What do you mean? Surely you can do it or you can't?'

'It's not that simple. For a start, I don't know how to bring a flame to life from nothing. It's part of why I came to the city—to seek a tutor.' *One I might still find,* he reminded himself. 'The first lesson of any magic use is that anything, no matter how small the act, requires energy, just like lifting an iron or chasing a loose pig. For example, if you were to hold a sack of grain to your chest, you might be able to for a time, perhaps even a dozen minutes. However, as soon as you hold that bag of grain at arm's length, the act becomes significantly more difficult, requiring more energy.' To demonstrate, his fork lifted into the air. At first, they had all jolted, surprised, but after a checking look to Eder, they awed at it, laughing in wonder. The fork twirled in the air, spiralling around the candle. Eder let it soar away from the table towards the fire. His brow furrowed, and as it moved further away from the table, the fork wobbled, then when he looked away, it clinked to the hearth as he let out a pent-up breath.

His spectators looked back, grinning, a round of applause arising from his efforts. Eder smiled, feeling more confident. 'I may not be able to conjure fire, but that's not to say I can't manipulate it.' His gaze flicked to the candle and the flame suddenly shot up going from the size of his nail to the length of his hand. He looked away again and it dropped to its former height.

A stunned look crossed Lucida's face, a realisation dawning on her. 'Hold on, when you caught me earlier, you didn't throw anything to trip me?' Eder grinned and relief swept across her. 'That means I've still never been caught,' she declared triumphantly.

'Just like you're not a criminal?' Eder smirked as the others shared his mirth.

Kaia held him in her sights, suddenly more serious. 'Tell me something, Eder. I've heard that using magic can kill the Maxia? Is that true?'

He frowned. 'Well, I'm not dead just yet, but yes. Imagine that instead of holding the bag of grain at arm's length, you have it balanced on the end of a shovel. That'd be hard, right? To sustain it. If I were to try to lift or move something that was on the outer wall from here, the energy required to do it would probably kill me. It's like that shovel's length is from here to the wall. I think only if I were to commit to the act then it would kill me, or if I were to try to do something that required too much energy, like stop a galloping horse.'

'Who taught you?' Lucida asked. 'You said you're looking for a teacher, but you seem to know plenty already.'

'What I know is similar to that of an apprentice smith in his first week. My Grand Pa was the one who taught me the laws of magic. He's a Maxia, but he keeps it hidden. He didn't use magic for years until I started showing some talent for it, though apparently, he is much weaker in it, now. He told me once that he used to be much stronger, and that he could have picked me up and held me in the air without even breaking a sweat. When he discovered the skill had been passed on, skipping a generation, he taught me all he could, but when one hasn't studied the skill, one can only teach the extent of their own knowledge.'

Lucida suddenly sat up. 'Can you teach me?'

He looked at her a moment, unsure if she were joking. 'As far as I know, it's usually passed along bloodlines.'

'I don't know my parents. We never met them. Maybe they were Maxia. Maybe it's why they hid Oskar and I.' She was getting more excited, shifting in her seat in earnest.

Eder paused a moment, then shrugged. *No harm in showing them how, I suppose.* He looked about the table, searching for something small. He plucked a berry from Hirst's plate. 'Hold this on your palm. You two can try, too, if you like,' he said, nodding to Kaia and Hirst. Lucida held her palm out flat, waiting for her next instruction. He checked the other two were ready. 'Before our language, magic was called *Votande,* or, *The Will.* It was called this because, like when moving a part of your body, you will it to do so. Using magic is just the same, you just are willing something to move without using your body.' He checked she was still following, then continued.

'It is as simple as *Willing* something to move, but it requires focus. Look at the berry and rid yourself of any other thought, any other distraction. Pay attention to no other sound, or motion, or itch. Focus on the berry. Let it consume your focus until nothing else is present. It'll take time, and practise to do swiftly, but once you've got that degree of focus, you can then command an object to move.'

He sat and watched for some moments, not moving. Each member of the table peered at their berry, eyes straining at it. If anyone walked into the room, they would have thought they had taken leave of their senses. Kaia was the first to give up, admitting defeat with the tip of a palm. Hirst followed soon after, tossing the berry back onto his plate. They all turned their attention to Lucida, the berry level with her eyes. She breathed slowly, rhythmically.

Suddenly, her hand twitched, making the berry roll. She shot to her feet. 'I did it,' she cried. 'I have magic!'

Kaia and Hirst burst out laughing. 'You moved,' Kaia giggled.

'I did not,' she said indignantly.

Eder couldn't keep the smirk off his face. 'Just keep trying—it's not something that always comes on the first attempt.'

Kaia shook her head, standing and setting a kettle of water over the hearth. 'How did you discover you could do it?'

'Use magic?' he said, looking over. He leaned back in his chair. 'Well, one day I sneezed, and fire shot out of my ass.' Everyone stopped and stared at him. He held a straight face for a moment, then broke out into laughter. 'I don't know, really. It's something I've been able to do for as long as I can remember. Grand Pa believes that everyone has it inside of them, and for

222

some, it has to be unlocked by some sort of experience. Everyone has moments of fear and panic in their childhood where they have to do something that will keep them alive. To me, magic is like another sense, another arm that has always been there, and to not use it would be like having an arm stuck in a sling.'

Hirst raised an eyebrow. 'Do you mind if I ask what happened that "unlocked" your magic?'

Eder pursed his lips. 'I'm not certain, but Grand Pa guessed it was when I fell. I'm from a coastal village, you see. Cliffs line the land before dropping away to the beach and the ocean. I was playing along the cliffs one day, climbing with a friend of mine. We used to do it all the time, even though we were told that it was dangerous. Sure, sometimes your grip slipped or the rock under your hand tore away, but usually the worst we got was a mouthful of dirt. Well, not that time. We were nearing the top, and when my hand slipped, I fell.'

The others stared at him, waiting. 'It was a hundred-foot drop and I don't remember what happened. My friend ran to get help, and I woke up several days later, exhausted and aching, but certainly not dead. Grand Pa reckons that just before I hit the ground, I used magic for the first time. I stopped myself from hitting the floor, pausing my descent just enough to save my life. I suffered no marks, no scratches or bruises. The people in my village called it a miracle, saying that Fate was not done with me yet.'

'That's incredible,' Kaia murmured.

Lucida only watched him. She, too, had been taken by the story, but he could see the disappointment on her face, and he found himself blundering for something to give her hope. The door opened before he could.

Leis strode into the room, fine clothes exchanged for something a little more humble with a thicker lining to it. He raised an eyebrow at the fork lying by the hearth but made no comment. Instead, he stood aside and let Oskar in. The boy refused to look at any of them, instead focussing on the floor. 'Whatever feelings you have,' Leis said, moving towards the table, 'set them aside. Tonight's the night. Eder, I want you to accompany the others. I wouldn't normally ask a new recruit to go, but considering your talents, you might prove yourself of value.'

Eder looked startled, unsure at the eagerness roused in Lucida and the others. 'Tonight's the night for what? What's happening?'

Lucida stood, a devilish spark in her eye. 'The jeweller's. We're going to steal the crown.'

Chapter XVII

Four dark figures marched ahead, hoods cloaking their features. Stars sparkled in the sky, the only other light sneaking out from behind shutters. There was a hushed conversation shared between them, and Eder remained as bewildered as he had been when he had first heard the plan.

They walked quickly, heading towards the inner walls. Few people were out, but those who were cast furtive glances their way, as if being noticed by the shadows would draw them near. One of the group dropped back, carrying a sack. They waited for Eder to catch up. It was Lucida. 'Feeling okay?'

'Nervous,' he admitted.

'You'll be fine. You're one of us, remember? Go over the plan one more time. It'll help.'

Eder chewed his lip, ordering events in his mind. 'If Kaia's contact was right, the shop owner will be out celebrating with some of his friends. There will be two guards on the inside, likely sleeping somewhere within the building. Hirst will unlock the doors, letting us in. We locate the guards, deal with them in whatever way is best, then find the safe, apparently in the back of the workshop. Hirst will work there. Kaia will be on the door, keeping look out. Once the safe's open, you'll take the crown, then we leave, split up, and meet back at the house.'

'See,' she said, trotting next to him, 'you'll be just fine.'

They passed under the shadow of the inner walls and Eder found himself shirking beneath it. Most of the houses were dark, the residents already asleep; Eder hoped the jewellers would be too.

Leis had explained that the jeweller was the best in the city, a mature man who had apprenticed under the palace's own smithy. He had apparently chosen to leave the service of the monarchy, hoping that his skills might be of interest to those beyond the royal courts. He had not been disappointed, but the crown had not let him from its grip entirely: he still worked for it foremost—these tasks taking priority over any other.

With the death of King Dessius, Kaia had been urged to keep a keen ear out for any news. Leis told them that he had been contacted, asking if he would be interested in the job. Their success would change the kingdom for the better, he said, and no longer would there be such a gulf between the rich and the poor; the people would become equal once more. The contact had not come to him directly, but a signed letter and a wax seal from a noble house had been enough. They were promised a fine reward: a house within the inner walls and enough coin that they need never want again.

Eder had refrained from asking what would happen if he had declined.

Once they had the crown, Leis would take care of matters from there. Beyond that, he was tight-lipped. He had formulated the plan, told them what to expect and the best way around obstacles, but he only told them what they needed to know in order to complete their part of the task.

Despite his apprehension, Eder was impressed. He could find no fault in the planning, though he wondered how long they had had to prepare, with the king's death only a short time ago. *Perhaps it had even begun before the king had been killed,* he had thought, but subdued the idea before he could dwell on it. He was simply doing as he was asked, becoming a part of their activities for a night. *Tomorrow I'll find my tutor,* he promised himself. *It's only for one night, then it can be forgotten. It'll be like some fanciful midnight dream.*

Kaia took the lead shortly after the inner walls, leading them further into the warren of alleys, winding discreetly through them. They stepped over a drunk, spooked a stray dog, then Kaia held her hand up, stalling them. She peeked her head around the corner, eyeing the street. She turned and faced them. 'The jeweller's is two doors down on the right. Hirst, you're up. You'll know if there's anything.' He nodded, not waiting: he knew the drill.

Eder watched him unroll his tool kit and get to work. His hands worked deftly; not even the chink of metal made its way around the corner. Oskar crossed the road, turned, and sat against a wall, letting his head loll. If anyone looked, he would be just another drunk. Looking closer, they would see his head tilted slightly, an eye maintained on Hirst. Eder retreated back into the alley and leaned against a wall, tapping his foot against the cobbles. He looked up to the sky, taking a breath to calm himself. A hand touched his shoulder, and Lucida gave him a smile.

Across the road, Oskar looked up, nodded, and climbed to his feet. Kaia led them into the street as Hirst held the door open. Oskar held back, and just before Eder stepped inside, Oskar caught his wrist. 'This goes wrong, and it's on you,' he whispered, glancing inside. 'You make a noise, or slow anyone down, and I'll know you're acting against us. These people are my family—you do anything that threatens them, and I'll make sure it's the last thing you do. Understand, rat?'

Eder flinched, snatched his hand back, and leaned closer. 'You could try, but if you did,' Eder clicked his fingers, '*poof.*' He smirked as he left Oskar staring after him.

The room was cold. The front of the building was occupied by the shop, and slanted table tops held an assortment of bracelets, rings, and necklaces; some hung around the necks of busts. Eder could see Lucida's hand itching, but she kept them by her side. Leis had made it clear that they take nothing else: they were there for one item only, and he had dismissed any argument otherwise. As Eder walked around, he realised the contents of the shop would have set them all for life, enough to exchange for a duke's ransom.

They dispersed throughout the room. One door led to a back room, another, to the right, led upstairs. The room to the back was unlocked and Hirst let himself through to attend to the safe; and Kaia took her post by the front door, leaving it ajar. She tossed the others a nod as she went, silently wishing them luck. Oskar looked at Eder and Lucida, lifted the latch, and slipped up the stairs. Eder squinted up the dark staircase, footsteps creaking the floorboards.

It was as Leis had foretold: there were two doors to the left, one to the right; the first on the left emitted the soft mutter of conversation, as well as a warm glow of light from around its borders. Oskar and Lucida met eyes and gestured for Eder to stand further down the corridor. Lucida placed the sack she had been carrying on the floor, and Oskar counted down from three on his fingers, but just before he knocked, Eder caught his fist. Oskar pulled back, giving him a sharp look, but Eder urged him to be still. He held a hand up, motioning for them to wait for his signal, then he lay on his chest and peered under the door. He made out a few shapes, discerning shadows. In the middle of the room, a table sat two pairs of feet. There was a bed, and what Eder guessed was a chest of drawers. He glanced back up to the others, held his hand up, and turned his focus back to the room. Closing his eyes, he counted down from three on his hand. As he shut his palm, he Willed his energy forward. A crash came from within the room, and a cry went up. Oskar threw the door open, and he and Lucida stormed the room. Eder dragged himself up, fetching himself up against the doorframe. Lucida was upon the first guard, his legs flailing in the air as he tried to gather himself. Oskar followed, leaping over a fallen chair and colliding with the other as he tried to stand, slamming him into the back wall. In the struggle, the guard knocked his head against the chest of drawers and his body went limp. Lucida struggled with the other as he flipped her onto her back, hands crushing her throat.

Eder took a step forward, but his vision swam and he gasped, trying to steady himself. Footsteps rattled up the stairs and Kaia pushed past, grabbing the sack as she went and spilling its contents. Oskar threw his body into the guard, sending them both sprawling, then Kaia grabbed the guard by his shoulders and hurled him against the wall. Lucida remained on the floor, heaving in gasps of air. 'Oskar,' Kaia said, holding her hand out. He tossed her a length of rope from the sack as she pressed the outer edge of her wrist against his windpipe. 'Lucida, get over here. Eder, suck it up and help Oskar.'

Eder nodded blindly, tottering forward before he fell onto his knees, fumbling with a length of rope. He wrapped it around the man's ankles, and he had to concentrate to secure the knot. Once bound, they trussed the guards behind the bed. Kaia was the first to go back down, returning to her post as sentry. Oskar gave Lucida a concerned glance before reassessing the knots. Eder felt his strength gathering slowly, but as he trod down the stairs, he leaned heavily against the railing that ran up the wall.

They convened in the back room. Eder left the others to talk in a hushed voices as Hirst worked with an assortment of tools around him. Occasionally, he would press his ear to the metal, his fingers adjusting to sounds beyond Eder's hearing.

Eder decided to leave him to his work; he had played his part, and he felt tired for it. Instead, he wandered the workshop. Aside from the workbench, the room was home to a stack of shelves, some containing books, others storing tools.

The workbench was an array of items: jewels and instruments littered the surface; a vice held a delicate, golden ring in place, whilst an embalming tool was discarded nearby. Eder paused to observe a small hammer, its head no larger than his thumbnail.

The door swung open. 'Guards on the street,' Kaia whispered. 'Why isn't that safe open?'

'I'm nearly there,' Hirst snapped. 'A few more minutes.'

She put Oskar and Eder in her sights. 'You two, with me. They're going to need as much time as we can buy. Lucida, as soon as that safe is open, you run. We'll meet back with Leis but remember to split up.' With that, she stole back into the front room. Eder followed Oskar, his eyes suddenly bright, alert. Kaia crouched in front of the door, peering through the crack between it and the doorframe.

In the gloom, none would discern the difference in the door. Oskar joined her, but Eder stood in front of the door, preferring not to see the guards as they walked past. He heard them, though, talking between themselves:

'—threw her in the cells. Saw it myself,' one gossiped.

'Think of throwing your own Ma in the cells, eh?' the other said, not hiding his disgust. They were level with the door for but a few seconds. Eder could hear the scuff of their boots on the stone, his heart thundering. Kaia held her breath and let it out once their voices had become more muted.

A clang made Eder jump, followed by the whining of metal against metal. He felt his face pale. Outside, the guards hesitated and turned towards the house. 'Best just make sure the old sod's alright,' the voice approached. 'So old I'm surprised he can still use his hands. Trembles like an autumn leaf, he does.'

The thudding of boots came from behind him and Eder heard a flurry of movement. Lucida came rushing through, a heavy sack in her arms. Kaia was on her feet, catching Lucida before she could burst through the door. She pressed a finger to her lips. Oskar closed his eyes, stood behind the door, and steeled himself, hand ready to pull it open. Kaia ushered the others back into the other room just as a knocking came from the door.

'Who is it?' Oskar replied, sounding flustered.

'Just the guard, Mister Russell. Everything okay?' The door pushed open slowly, and Oskar made as though he were just walking towards it.

'Yes, yes, everything's fine. Just knocking over some things walking about in the dark. Fate forbid Master Russell ever kept candles.' Eder could hear his guilty grin.

'Who're you?'

'Master Russell's apprentice, sir. Anything I can do for you?'

'Mister Russell has no apprentice.'

'Started this week, sir. Still settling into my habits. Not quite sure how Master Russell likes his workshop left.'

'In one piece, I imagine,' he said, his voice riddled with suspicion.

The other spoke up. 'Wasn't the crown here to be remedied for the king?'

'How did you hear that? That's supposed to be secret—though wouldn't do much good knowing it. No one alive can open that bloody safe.'

Eder pressed himself against the wall, hoping they would not want evidence. 'You know,' the first voice said, 'I've heard it from Russell himself. Said he'd never take an apprentice in Corazin. Wanted to move away before he did.' The scepticism made Eder's stomach knot. 'Come with us, lad. Think we need to ask Mister Russell a few questions, don't you?'

'Now, I hardly think that's necessary. It's late, and Mr Russel would be furious if we interrupted his evening for such a trivial matter.' The sound of a sword being drawn sent a chill down Eder's spine.

'Go,' Kaia yelled, charging from around the corner. The guard already had the tip of his sword directed to Oskar's chest. The swordsman jolted, then thrust the sword forward. Eder reacted through instinct, Willing the sword upwards, but he was too slow. The sword was sent skewering, but not high enough. It tore a gash through Oskar's shoulder, and had Eder not intervened, Oskar would already be dead. Instead, the sword thudded into the doorframe, lodging itself there. The other guard had retreated, sword drawn. In the confusion, Kaia barged past, as did Lucida. They broke off in separate directions. Eder could only watch, the effort it had taken to divert the blade making his head swim again. Hirst gave him a shove, propelling him sideways.

With a final yank, the guard pulled his blade free, letting Hirst speed past him whilst his companion shook himself and took off after Lucida. 'She's taken something,' he cried.

The other guard blocked the doorway, trapping Eder and Oskar. The older boy was clutching his shoulder, cursing loudly.

'Alright, lads,' the guard said calmly, eyeing them up. 'Looks like your game's over. Come with me, and no one else gets hurt.'

Eder glanced between him and Oskar, trying to draw Oskar's attention. The guard took a step inside, filling the exit. Eder leaped forward, grabbed Oskar and pulling him behind him so that Eder was stood in front protectively.

'Come now,' the guard grinned menacingly. 'You're trapped, lad. No weapon. Nothing to defend yourself. There's no way you're getting away.'

Gritting his teeth, Eder knew he was right. He watched as the man took another step inside. The chair nearest to him flipped through the air, striking him in the chest and knocking him backwards. It was a poor effort, and the man's armour provided ample protection from the blow, but the distraction was enough. Eder charged him, lowering his shoulder to force him back into the street. The guard tumbled backwards, rolled to his feet and hefted the sword, snarling. Eder looked back to the building. Oskar was still clutching his shoulder, stumbling for the door. 'Hurry up,' Eder yelled, but he knew Oskar was going nowhere fast.

The guard grinned, seemingly appreciative of the challenge. 'Maxia swine. The king'll be pleased to see your head.' He darted forwards, making to cut across Eder's ribcage. Eder rolled off to the side, keeping himself between the guard and Oskar. He could hear Oskar shuffling along, but dared not look back, lest his opponent take his chance.

Again, the guard stormed forward, blade swinging. Eder could do little but duck and roll away, knowing his luck would only last so long. Before he could find some sort of weapon to defend himself, the guard advanced again, unrelenting. Just as he was rolling away again, the blade jabbed forward and tore into his leg. A burning pain slashed across his calf and he groaned, stilling him mid-roll.

The guard loomed over him, a wicked smile on his face. 'Not going anywhere now, are you? You just wait here, I'll go and get that friend of yours.'

He turned his back and started walking down the street, twirling his sword as he went. Oskar had not made it far, and Eder scrambled for an idea. He came to a single solution. He closed his eyes, focussed, and blotted out the throbbing in his leg. When he opened his eyes again, he watched the sword swing lightly in the guard's grip, the guard further than he had realised. He Willed it mid-flourish. The blade spun, pulling out of the guard's hand, and burying into his thigh, erupting out the other side again.

Normally, such a task would not have cost him much, but at such a distance, and already weakened from his earlier efforts, Eder slumped into the floor, his vision blurring. The guard fell to the ground, crying out, but Eder squinted, trying to discern the figure stumbling further away before it slipped into an alley. In an effort to stop his head spinning, he closed his eyes, ignoring the thudding in his chest and the general exhaustion that overcame him.

The darkness began to spin, and he spiralled with it.

Eder fell in and out of consciousness. He knew that someone had come to investigate the noise, and seeing the guard on the floor, decided to follow his instruction of finding reinforcements. When he woke the second time, he was inside the jewellers again, the guards that had been tied up now loose. They muttered among themselves, but Eder struggled to make sense of it.

'—back to the palace. It'll be safer there. Get Kile patched up.'

'And him?'

'Throw him in the cells. Let the rats chew through him for all I care. We've got enough on our hands tonight.'

'He's a Maxia. The king will want to see him.'

'Raiden is scared shitless already. Chuck him in the cells—we'll tell the king in the morning. The kid looks half-dead anyway.'

'Any others?' this voice seemed to struggle, as though sucking in breaths caused a fresh dose of discomfort.

'No, but we got what's most important.'

Then he had felt hands on him, someone trussing him over their shoulder, and jolting movements returned him to a safe, discreet darkness. He lingered there, reluctant to come out. Here, he could not feel the aches and discomforts of his body, nor the wound on his leg. Instead, he was content to sit and exist for a while, weaving his way in and out of delirium.

Chapter XVIII

A presence brushed his mind, and he opened his eyes. He was lying on the floor. It was dark. Walls were near, but he struggled to care. He receded back into his mind. At first, he had thought it was the crocodile, but whilst the crocodile had been dominating, this one seemed to gently encircle him, toeing its way around the periphery of his mind. He shrunk back further, not wishing to be disturbed.

As though in reaction, the presence surrounded and engulfed him. He gasped at the vibrancy of it, at the sheer power it exhumed. *You cannot wallow in this pit for long. It is too cold, and you'll find nothing of interest. Also, you need a bath.*

Eder groaned, sitting up. *Who are you? Look, I can't help. I need to sleep.'*

The voice belonged to a female, and the more he hid from it, the more she seemed to pull at him, tugging at the parts of him that he curled away from her.

You can't get out of your cell if you stay like this, can you?

Cell? I'm in a cell… he realised. *Why would I want to get out of my cell?*

Would you rather hang?

He paused.

Eder, you are a Setter. The paths change and are laid before your feet. Wherever you walk, other paths converge, seeking to pull themselves as close to yours as they can. Your path is the path that leads.

But I want to sleep, he thought, struggling to find the effort to reply. *Did you speak to the crocodile?*

Crocodile? Do you often speak to crocodiles? I was informed of you by an ally—a man we both know well. Our kind need protecting, just as we protect those who need it.

I don't understand….

Perhaps if you wake up, you'll see more than the dismal recesses of your mind. You're becoming undone, Eder. Dwell here too long, and you may find it hard to come back. The kingdom teeters with you. Whichever way you fall, your kingdom will fall alike, but know this: the queen is your friend. Use her knowledge, listen to her words. Now, wake!

The presence disappeared, and he jolted awake, instantly groaning in regret at the pain from his leg. He was strewn on the concrete floor of a cell. His body ached, tongue dry. To his surprise, someone had already tended to his wound, bandaging his leg, though it still throbbed as much as his head. He climbed onto his hands and knees, whimpering to himself. There was a bench and a bucket. Nothing else. His tongue felt dry and, despite the woman's warning, panic kicked at his chest as he noticed the door with a barred window.

'Hello? Are you awake?' A voice came somewhere outside, and Eder squeezed his eyes shut. *Is that the same voice as in my dream?*

'Hello?'

No, it's different. He made to speak, but his voice rasped out as a whisper.

'I know you're there. Please, just wake up.'

Eder cleared his throat and crawled to the bench, using it to lift himself up. He swayed on his feet a moment, then shuffled to the door, not putting weight on his leg. 'Are you talking to me?'

'Yes,' the voice cried. 'Oh, yes. I'm so glad you're awake. When the guards brought you in, I thought you were as good as dead.'

Eder grunted. 'Not quite.' He sighed and looked around. 'Have I been here long? Has there been anyone else?'

'No,' she said, 'just you. You are the first person I have seen since my— since I was thrown in here.'

He slouched against the wall. *At least that means they got away.*

'They were talking about how they got something back, though. I'm not sure what it was, but one of them was very angry with you. He wanted to have you executed tonight.'

Eder straightened. 'They got something back? Are you sure?' He wondered how Lucida had escaped yet also lost the crown. He felt his face pale as he realised the alternative. 'Did they say anything else?'

'Not that I heard. What did you do to anger them so?'

He chuckled uncomfortably. 'I put a sword through one of their legs during a—' he stopped himself. 'It doesn't matter. I wounded the guard before he could catch my friend.'

'A noble sacrifice,' she commented.

Eder snorted and turned his back to the wall, speaking into the room. 'You know, if you'd told me yesterday that I'd be locked up with a hole in my leg, I'd have told you you'd lost your senses.'

'A short criminal career, then?'

'You could say that,' he smiled. 'What about you? Why are you here?'

'My son. He's...' she paused, and when she resumed, she seemed less certain of herself. 'I'm a maid, you see. In the palace. I was caught stealing a candelabra—though I doubt anyone would ever have missed it. Beastly things.'

Eder nodded to himself, though he cared little for the candelabras himself. He hoped the others had made it safely back, that Oskar was being treated. Closing his eyes, Eder tried to order his priorities, starting with himself. 'The guards talked about an execution.... They weren't serious, were they?'

'You attacked a guard,' she said bluntly.

'Right,' he said. *I can't stay here a moment longer then.*

'You're not from Corazin, are you?'

'No,' he frowned, gripping the bars of the door as he tried to peer down the corridor. Torches hung along the walls, casting a weak glow beyond his cell. Aside from that, there was no other light.

'What is your name?'

'Eder,' he said, absent-mindedly. 'Call me Ed. What's yours?'

The lady hesitated again, letting him focus on the shadows as he tried to discern whether there was anyone else in the hallway, though he reasoned that if there were, they would have been ordered to silence by now.

He crouched by his door, balancing on one leg as he peered through the crease between the door and the doorframe.

'Selina,' she said decisively. Suddenly, her voice was serious. She spoke quickly, commanding. 'Listen, Ed. A rebellion is on its way. Tonight. A friend came to me earlier and I promised her that we would escape. She said the walls of the city will be breached, and the palace will burn. We cannot stay here. I dread to think what would come of us if they found us here.'

He paused, pulling himself back. 'A rebellion?' he said curiously. *If there's enough of a distraction, I might still be able to get hold of the crown, then I'd never have to worry about Leis again.* 'Did you have a plan?'

She sighed, and her voice grew fainter as she walked away from the door. 'I do not. I might have been able to once, but….'

Eder stood, keeping his weight off of his injured leg. *If she's worked inside the palace, she'll know where to look.* 'Selina, you were a maid, right? How much of the palace do you know?'

'Every corner of every chamber.'

He pursed his lips. 'If I asked you to help me, would you be able to take me to somewhere?'

'You want to go back to the palace?' she said incredulously. 'The guard will be on high alert with the attack and the rebels so near. Raiden and Islo will have everyone on duty. There would be no way.'

'The attack? And who are—' he cut himself off. 'Listen, all I need you to do is show me where to go. Once that's done, we can leave. You can go wherever you want.'

For a time, there was no response and Eder grew impatient. He sighed, pressed his hand against the door, and shut his eyes. A clang resounded around his cell and he pushed the door open. The corridor was long and ended with a wall at either side, though a staircase, he assumed, must have been near one. A pair of eyes looked out at him from behind a set of bars, shocked. 'How did you—'

The sound of a ringing bell shoved into the corridor. At first, he paused to listen. *Come on,* he rolled his eyes. *I'm barely out of my cell.* The clanging multiplied rapidly, picking up voices and gaining volume, reverberating around the stone dungeon until it was the only sound he could hear.

'Are you going to help me?' he said over the din. She had blond hair and round eyes. She wore a thin night shift, and her fingers shook with cold.

'How did you do that?' she demanded.

'Answer the question, or I'll have to leave you.'

Her eyes widened, and she took a step back. 'You're one of... *them*.'

He rolled his eyes. 'Yes, I can use magic. I guess that means you're staying put.' He turned to leave, but her voice caught his shoulder.

'I'll help you,' she said hurriedly, 'but only if you answer me this. Did you murder my husband?'

'What? No, why would I want to do that? I've never killed anyone, and I don't intend to.'

She gave him a level stare, lips thin. She nodded. Eder flicked his eyes to the door and the latch clanked open. She pushed the door tentatively, as though not believing it were true. She looked up to him, not moving from the cell, trepidation clear on her face. He started limping down the hall, ignoring the pain in his leg as best he could, but she stopped him. 'The stairs are this way, Ed.'

He cringed inwardly but turned and walked past her without a word. She strode to his shoulder. 'If I am to guide you, it may be worthwhile that I know where you wish to be guided.'

'I need to steal the crown,' he said flatly.

She grabbed his wrist and, with surprising strength, spun him around. He struggled to maintain his balance on his good leg. 'You're with Leis?' she asked.

He stared at her, snatching his wrist back. 'How do you know that name?'

The flicker of a smile touched her lips and she shook her head in disbelief. 'I knew he was clever, but a Maxia? Well played, Leis.'

Glaring at her, he narrowed his eyes. 'How do you know Leis? And I'm not one of his.'

She shook her head, walking ahead of him, though the amusement was undisguised. 'I hired him.'

Eder faltered. 'What does a maid want with a crown?'

'You could say Leis and I are old friends. He is a man who knows how to get things done.'

He raised an eyebrow. 'And maids need help with that?'

She dismissed him swiftly. 'So, Ed, where is Leis meeting you? I thought his troops were never caught.'

She hurried up the steps and halted at a door. There was an abandoned chair next to it and the door hung ajar. Eder peered out, ignoring the comment as he spied people running and hurrying about, shouting insensibly. The maid hung back and looked to him. 'Walk confidently, keep your head down, and I'll take you there, but there's one thing.' She looked at him sternly. 'I need to find my son. I need him to leave this city with me before he gets hurt.'

He studied her for a moment, then nodded, deciding he had little other choice. With the confirmation, she strode out into the street, shoulders back, chin held high. He wondered why she had not taken her own advice, but he was reluctant to question her. They made their way towards the palace, no one pausing for a second glance. Bodies rushed from house to house, shouting to one another. Guards gave orders and seemed just as panicked; Eder was sure he had never seen such chaotic activity, and comparing it to earlier, much of it was flitted with uncertainty instead of the focussed and determined people he had taken for Corazin's folk.

The doors were open as people were evacuated from the palace and stowed away. Eder kept his head ducked as Selina led him through a great garden filled with trees and flowers. If it had been daylight, Eder thought he would have liked to stop and admire it for a time, but instead, the maid hurried him up to a set of double doors. Checking he was behind her, Selina nudged the door open and peered inside. Akin to beyond the palace walls, people rushed from room to room, servants and handmaids burdened high with the belongings of nobles and guests. The roofs were higher than Eder had ever seen, with the walls painted a deep gold. Art and flowers sat near the walls, all of them flawless.

They took a left, seeking shelter behind a pillar. Selina crouched beside him and spoke just so he could hear, though had the gongs not thrummed through the air her voice would have been heard by those stood near the doors at the end of the hall.

'This is where we must part ways. My son is in the chambers here, most likely the library. You must go across the hall to the council's offices. The crown will likely be in one of them. I will meet you here shortly. If I do not come, go on without me. I will do the same in similar circumstances.'

Eder gave her a curt nod before she spun and hurried into the gloomy halls beyond, jumping over something on the floor as she crossed the threshold.

Eder looked directly across the hall. There was an identical door there, and after a look, he stalked across, keeping his eyes set on the door.

Within the hall, torches hung along the walls, casting dancing shadows and wobbling silhouettes. *Where do I start?* He stopped by the first door but found it already ajar. Pushing it open only revealed a slept-in bed and warm coals on the fire. The next two rooms were similar, all betraying the fact that their residents had left in a hurry. After these, the rooms changed to offices, containing desks and ink wells, books and sheaves of paper. He inspected these rooms closer, stepping into some, trying not to be drawn by the artwork housed within, especially that of a painting of the city. Somehow, the artist had managed to capture the grandeur of the city whilst retaining the understanding that all within were segregated, the boundaries of one wall a clear boarder. The structure seemed a pimple of power within an otherwise empty landscape, and this power had come to sour those who wielded it.

The next door he tried was locked. He stood back and examined it. *Well, now what?*

You're a Maxia, aren't you, a voice startled him. *You must be calm, Setter, and perhaps learn to guard your mind. You have a gift. Now is the time to use it.* It was the same voice from his dream, yet whilst he shirked from it, he realised there was no fleeing from it. It was able to rifle through every emotion he felt, responding to each as though assessing him.

'Who are you?'

There is a time for questions another day, Setter. For now, you must make sure you see another day to ask them. Do as you have always done. Use your gift, embrace it and hide it no longer.

He frowned, shaking his head. He pressed his hand to the door and shut his eyes, focussing on the wood beneath his fingers. He reduced his focus to a specific bump under his thumb, then Willed the lock to move. A clunk shuddered through the wood and his hand hurried to the handle to push it open. This room was cold, though dressed similarly to the others. Moonlight beamed in through a window and spilled across the desk, allowing him to navigate the room with ease. Whilst the art surrounding him was just as remarkable as in the others, it was the ornament on the desk that caught his eye. Wrought from gold and encrusted with precious stones, the crown gleamed. Next to it, the sack Lucida had been carrying.

Pushing away any concerns, he slipped the crown into the sack and made for the door, just has he heard hurried footsteps and voices approaching.

Remember, the voice said within him, *fight smartly, and you'll win every time.*

A man's voice came from the hall. 'Why are we left here to protect some bloody office? The action's out there.'

'Because every time you pick up a damned sword you're just as likely to cut your own arm as your enemy's.' According to the other man's tone, it wasn't the first time the topic had been addressed.

Eder stood in the office, floundering. There was little else in the room aside from the desk and shelves, much less something to hide behind. When the door swung open, he was stranded in the middle and swords were drawn.

'What's this, then? A thief?' The older of the pair, the latter speaker, watched him carefully, allowing room for the other guard to enter. The first held his sword at arm's length, the other held his sword with a limp wrist, facing Eder squarely.

His tongue flopped in his mouth like an old piece of leather. 'No, sir. I was sent to fetch this.' Eder plucked a sheet of paper with writing scribbled across it from the desk.

'Bit old for a page, aren't you?'

'An apprentice, sir. Learning the scribe's trade.' The older man narrowed his eyes, so Eder pressed on. 'Read it for yourself,' he said, thrusting the paper forward. 'I was asked to bring it before dawn, so my master might work as soon as he rouses, but in his rush to safety, he forgot it and sent me.'

The guard took it, his eyes scanning the paper. Eder guessed he knew as much about his letters as Eder did. 'And who's your master?'

Eder waited until he glanced at the paper, the slightest distraction, before he moved. He grabbed a quill from the desk and hurled it towards the guard. Had he not guided it with magic, it would have hit him in the chest, if that. Instead, Eder Willed the quill to a specific destination, retaining the force he had thrown it with. The guard stumbled back, crying out as he clutched at his eye. Blood ran down his cheek.

The younger guard had his sword raised to shoulder height, and he was arcing it towards Eder with a yell. His movements were deliberate, but seemingly slow. Eder took a deft step backwards as the sword slashed down in front of him, continuing with force into the wooden planks, embedding itself with a *thunk*.

They exchanged a glance, the guard dumbfounded that his attack had been dodged. Eder grabbed a paperweight—a metal prism—and charged him, tackling him to the ground. Although the guard was heavier, Eder had surprise to his advantage, enough to slam the paperweight into his temple. The body beneath him went limp and Eder rolled off, ready for the next.

The older guard was groaning, half of his face smeared with blood, as was his hand. The quill still remained lodged in his eye, and the sight made Eder wince. *It's him or me,* he reminded himself. The guard stood swaying, but his eye followed him, sword raised. 'You can't live, thief. You're dead,' he spat.

'I'll take my chances,' Eder said. The guard lurched forward, leading with the blade in a hope to spear him, though with only the single eye, his coordination was off. He lunged to Eder's shoulder, meaning Eder needed do no more than step aside. Eder left his foot trailing, hooking the guard's ankle and sending him sprawling. He watched a moment as the guard struggled, but his recovery was slow. Eder scooped up the bag and tugged the sword free of the wooden planks, then dropped it by the door. He shut it behind him, took a breath, and focussed. Behind the wood, a thud sounded as the blade embedded itself into the floorboards, the handle now wedged firmly against the door. The force he needed to push the blade deep enough surprised him, but he gave the door an experimental push, and it held.

Tossing the bag over his shoulder, he strolled down the corridor, retreating the way he had come and keeping as much weight on his good leg as possible. He passed no one, assuming they had all fled to defend the city. He peered out into the Great Hall and suppressed a groan. A contingent of guards stood before the closed doors of the palace, weapons drawn, each shifting nervously from foot to foot. None of them bothered to look behind, but Eder knew he could not meet Selina here. Scurrying from the door to a pillar, he peered around to the cohort again, realising that many of them were older guards, their muzzles greying. They were just another obstacle. Perhaps the hope was that they could present a challenge to the rebels who made it that far, tired from battling their way through the city.

Eder ducked his head, counted to three, then stole across the hall, sure to keep his steps light. The door of the opposing corridor was already open, but he nearly slipped as he crossed through it, his foot sliding. He caught himself, groaning as he stifled a yell when he jarred his leg. The ground felt slick, yet sticky if undisturbed. Peering closer, the gloom revealed a dark, viscous liquid. Eder did not linger any longer. He hurried down the corridor, immediately noticing the grandeur of the hall in comparison to the other. Here, sculptures and busts were intermittent; paintings of landscapes and battles lined the walls beside torches. He slowed as he neared a junction, another corridor crossing in front of it. Peering up and down, he saw it was clear, save for an object at the end of the corridor to his right.

He listened, keening his ears to any sound, hoping for Selina's voice. Instead, another carried itself down the corridor from an open door. Beyond the object on the floor, light streamed from a corner room. With a quick glimpse around him, he approached it, keeping a wary eye on the shadow. As he came closer, he realised it was the body of a dog, though its ribcage was still. *What's happened here?*

Words became audible from the room ahead. 'What would Father say?'

'Your father was killed by the same people who are ransacking the streets and setting buildings ablaze. They are here for *you*, Raiden.' It was Selina. Eder stepped nearer, realising too late that the corridor took a sharp left turn. Gathered around the corner, four tall, broad-shouldered men wearing black armour leaned against the wall.

One of them let out a shout while another started towards him. Eder made to turn and run, but a weight crashed into him, sending him careening to the tiled floor, the bag spilling from his grip. The body crushed the air out of his lungs, and when it rolled off of him, he gasped for air. Hands grabbed him by the scruff of his shirt and lifted him clear from the ground. 'It's a kid,' he said.

The other collected the bag and peered inside. 'A thief more like. Take a look.'

The guard's lips twisted, and he dropped Eder, letting him crumple as another gave him a sharp kick. 'Let's see what the king makes of this.' He shoved Eder towards the door, sending him half-sprawling into the warmly lit room.

The four shadows followed him, blocking his retreat. The room was a library, with a great hearth and walls lined with books. Selina stood, her back to Eder as a boy with curly blond hair faced the fire. When Selina heard them enter, she spun. 'I thought I told you to wait out—' She faltered when she saw Eder.

'My king,' one of the guards said, holding the bag in front of him. 'He had the crown.'

'You see,' the boy cried, finger pointed at Eder. 'They are upon us already. My Última Sombra protect us and you would have me flee? I am safer in their protection. I'm going nowhere.'

'He is no rebel,' she sighed. 'He is with me.' Eder thought he heard her mutter something about Leis, but the boy's surprise overwhelmed it.

'With you? You're colluding with the rebels?'

She gave him a look as though he had suggested that if he jumped from the outer wall that he would fly. 'He is working for the crown.'

'I am?' Eder said, confused, then his eyes widened. 'You're the queen? Queen Serana?' He dropped to his knee, head bowed. She shot him a look that told him she was finished with him until she spoke to him again. He hobbled to his feet and took another look at the woman. This was not the Selina he had met in the cells, and having changed from her night clothes, she seemed stronger. Standing in the heat of the fire, she seemed to thrive, exhuming authority.

'Raiden, my son, you must listen. The city *will* fall. If you stay, they will show no mercy.'

He scowled at her. 'Perhaps I should have done the same for you. This is treason, Mother. I will not flee my city like a timid child. I will stand and fight for my people.'

'Then you will be cut down with them,' she said sternly, speaking as though alone.

Raiden glowered. 'You said you believed that all would prosper beneath my reign.'

'How can a dead king prosper? I also said that you lead with your heart, not your mind. Whilst I don't doubt your heart is honourable, it is your mind that will keep you alive.'

A boom thundered from outside. The guards spun and turned to face the sound. Voices echoed down the hall and the guards drew their swords. 'Stay inside. None will pass, my king.' The door closed behind them.

'They are outnumbered,' Serana said gravely.

'Then they will die for their king,' Raiden said, a snarl on his lips.

Eder saw her sigh again, the defeat as plain as the heart-break. 'Come, Ed. We must take our leave.'

He scooped up the sack and hurried across the room, but the boy drew his sword and pointed it at him. 'Drop the crown. What king would I be without a crown?'

'A dead one. I am taking the crown so that Corazin may yet see another sit the throne.' She stood between the blade and Eder, letting him move behind her. The boy stared at his mother, then lowered his arm, glowering at her. She studied him a moment longer, then went to the corner of the room, pressed part of a flagstone, and a section of the wall jolted open, startling Eder. 'Go on,' she said softly, before addressing Raiden. 'This is your last chance. Come with me, my son. Better to flee now and reclaim your kingdom than to die and lose everything your ancestors have worked for.'

'I will not be known as the king who fled.' He turned to face the door, his sword drawn. 'Goodbye, Mother.'

'Men and their bloody honour.' She slammed the door shut, jarring them into pitch darkness. Eder felt his way along the wall for a short time, before her voice snapped, making him jump. 'Well?'

'Well, what?' he replied sheepishly.

'I can see just as little as you and these tunnels are a maze.'

He hesitated a moment, understanding what it was she asked. A boom sounded from beyond the door, followed by a series of shouts. They stood in silence, listening, holding their breath. There was a commotion, then a cheer. Eder heard the queen release a shaky breath.

I can do this, he said, composing himself. He held out his palm, though he couldn't see it. He closed his eyes, not to block anything out, but to envisage a flame on his palm.

He thought back to Grand Pa's lesson. 'Imagine you can see the air,' he had said, puffing on his pipe. 'To make a flame, you must move the air around a minute, focussed point, creating a tiny orb of speeding, spinning air.' Eder had sat and stared at his hand, moving rushing air above his palm, but only heat had grown. Grand Pa had stopped him every few minutes, offering him a pie or an apple with each pause. 'Gathering the flame is the hardest part. Once you have it, it is much easier to feed. Now focus, Ed. Try again.'

Eder took a breath, and focussed on his palm, though he could not see it in the darkness of the tunnel. Heat grew above his palm, but he retained his focus, holding the image in his mind and Willing the air to move faster. Suddenly, the heat bloomed to something stronger, and when he opened his eyes a flame the size of his fingernail flickered. He fed more air into the orb, elated as it grew slightly. It was only small, but his chest swelled with pride. *If only Grand Pa could see this.*

'Is that it?' Serana asked.

'This is the best I can do,' he said, trying not to feel dejected.

Be careful, the female voice cautioned in his mind again. *Do not over exert yourself. You are no use to anyone if you black out again. Feed the flame only enough to light your way and no more.*

'Where does Leis find you people,' she muttered. 'It will do. You lead, I will direct you.'

They set off, Eder grimacing with each step but maintaining his focus on the flame. In his periphery, brick walls blurred by, unchanging. Occasionally it was broken by another chamber, but they rarely turned, winding through a seemingly endless warren of tunnels. The sheer scale of it stunned Eder, as though an entire network lived beneath the streets. Every scuff of the boot and every stumble echoed ten-fold. Serana gave her instructions flatly, and when he asked where they were going, her only reply was to Leis.

Chapter XIX

Eder had little idea of how much time had passed in the tunnels, but his feet were sore and the effort from sustaining the flame had made him sweat and his body ache from tiredness. It became no more than a subtle glow by the end of their journey, enough to see the walls around them and little else.

When they finally surfaced, he tried to figure out how far away morning was. The night sky was no longer black, but a gloomy blue: the sun was on the approach. This had held his attention for but a moment.

Beneath the stars, the city burned. Thatch roofs were now ash and the flames had spread on the wind, carrying cinders from one to the next. Much of the southern and eastern sides were tall plumes of black smoke with the occasional hue of flames. The north was untouched, as was the inner circle of the city, which had tiled roofing.

The streets were deserted. Not even strays or beggars huddled in the alleys. There were no lights behind shutters, and as far as Eder could see, they walked in a city of ghosts. They hurried past a gate to the inner wall, when Serana stopped in her tracks.

'What? Who's there?' Eder said, peering over her shoulder. Something in the passage under the inner wall had caught her attention. There was a head mounted on a spike, and Eder looked away, grimacing.

'I knew him,' she said distantly. 'He was a good man....' She shook herself and led him quickly through a couple of streets before Eder recognised the dilapidated shell of the house, surprised at how little time it had taken them. She strode up to it, knocked in a pattern, and waited.

'Where are the guards?' he asked.

'Fighting,' she said without looking at him. 'Probably nearer the southern gates.' Her lips set to a straight line. 'Or hiding.'

The door cracked open and Serana rolled her eyes, pushing it open, sending whoever was behind it stumbling. 'If someone was going to break in, do you really think they would knock?' She strode to the kitchen as Hirst chased after her, making demands that she couldn't just walk in. Eder followed, seemingly unnoticed.

'Leis,' she said loudly, attracting the attention of everyone in the room. They sprang to their feet from chairs around the table. Lucida was the only one standing, her eyes red. Leis remained seated, continuing to brood next to the flames of the hearth. 'You promised me you could do this.'

He looked up and away from the fire, though flames still jumped in his stare. 'You could have at least told me the rebels were attacking tonight. We nearly lost…' he trailed off, eyes settling on the boy behind her. 'Eder? How did you—'

'Attack or no, your success would have been the same. You need not be privy to every whisper that comes my way. Fortunately, Ed here managed to get himself arrested and was able to set us both free.'

At the mention of Eder's name, Oskar twisted further from the table to look at him, though instead of disgust, as Eder had expected, the boy looked over him with a note of concern. His shoulder was bandaged and his arm in a sling, but aside from that, he was well.

'Serana, my queen,' Leis said. 'I'm sorry, but the crown was taken from us. We did all we could, but it was lose the crown, or hang.'

Eder wondered why he did not name Lucida as the guilty party, but the way she bowed her face and hid behind a curtain of loose hair proved her guilt. To the side, he saw Hirst lean to Kaia, asking if she was *the* Serana. She nodded, not taking her eyes from the scene.

'Then perhaps you should have chosen the rope. Had Fate taken another path, you would have found it a kinder mercy.' Leis stood, outrage making his lips twitch, but she lifted a hand to silence him. 'Eder has proven himself, and he has paid any debts to you ten-fold. She stood back and nodded to Eder. He dragged the crown out, letting the bag fall as he held it in both hands. Gasps went around the room, joined by a shout of elation. 'It seems I have done your task for you, Leis,' she continued. 'Expect no payment for your failure. I trust you kept your other promises?'

He regarded her a moment and nodded. 'The horses are beyond the walls to the north, as promised, my queen. Your handmaid will meet you with the others. It is safer for her to be as far from the city as possible.'

'Is there any word from Kerrick?'

'He will be there, my queen.' He frowned a moment, pursed his lips. 'Forgive me, Serana, but where is Raiden?'

A dark look came across Serana's face and Eder knew he immediately regretted asking. 'My son is with his father now.'

'I am sorry, Serana. Truly.' He bowed his head, but she made no sign of emotion nor acknowledgement. 'So, the heir to the throne....'

'We continue as planned. This simply means my reign will be longer than a regency. I'll return with the summer. Do not expect to hear from me before then.' She looked at the faces around the room, pausing on each. 'May your path be true, and your journey clear. All of you. Ed, leave the crown with Leis.'

He placed the crown on the table. As soon as he did, the voice returned. *Tell the queen you will accompany her, and that Kerrick has invited a guest to travel with her.*

Would you stop that? You can't just appear in my mind whenever you wish.

Can I not? Until you have been trained, anyone can. Be swift, Setter.

I need to make a stop.

The crocodile?

I have questions. I won't be long.

He sensed her acceptance, and she receded from his mind.

'My queen,' he started.

'Ed, I am not your queen. You are from another kingdom, and I do not rule here. For now, anyway.'

'Apologies, Selina—Serana,' he flushed, correcting himself. 'I would come with you. A man named Kerrick has a guest. She is why I came to Corazin. We will accompany you.'

She raised an eyebrow, looking at him sceptically.

'You can't go,' Lucida blurted. 'We need you here. We'll never be hungry again.'

Serana gave her a soft smile. 'I fear there will be many in this city who will go hungry in the coming seasons.'

Leis nodded, lighting his pipe. 'Aye, I'll be sad to see you go, Eder. Yet, a deal is a deal, and you have far surpassed your end of the bargain. Here, there's food inside,' he said, lifting Eder's rucksack from next to his chair. 'I hope what you have learned with us may come in useful one day, and should you ever need shelter or help, you are always welcome among us.'

Eder bowed. 'Thank you. Your kindness is generous.'

Serana turned on her heel. 'We must not tarry. This city is no longer safe.'

Oskar snorted. 'As if it ever was.'

She narrowed her eyes at him and he shrunk back against the table. She left without another word. Eder lingered a moment. 'May your paths be ever true, my friends.'

'And your journey clear, Eder,' Leis said, puffing at his pipe.

'Wait,' Lucida said, crossing the room. She threw her arms around his neck and embraced him. He grunted at the weight on his leg, but he held her equally tightly. 'Be safe,' she whispered, 'and come back soon. We still have a score to settle, you know.'

He nodded, remembering the competition she had proposed, and she let him go. Smiles met him as he looked around, then, with a final farewell, he left. Serana was stood outside, arms folded across her chest. 'It'll be daybreak soon. We must be swift.'

'I'll meet you beyond the walls,' he said, earning him a doubtful look.

'Where are you going?'

'I have a personal errand to run, first. I will catch up to you before you get there.'

She eyed him but sighed. Suddenly, she looked tired, as though any argument had left her. 'Go then and try to avoid getting arrested again.'

'You too,' he grinned, and he saw a sparkle of amusement in her eye. They went separate ways as he tried to recall the route to *The Heart's Whittler.*

Chapter XX

The store front was gloomy, dark, but similar to any other on the street. Herbs still swung in the breeze from the rafters and Eder tried the door handle. He felt daft being surprised at it being locked, but he unlocked it quickly. Creeping inside, he shut the door silently. 'Hello?' he whispered, but no one replied. The shop stunned him.

It was empty.

He looked around the empty tables, wondering how the shop's contents could possibly have been cleared in such a short time. Retracing his steps, he breathed in the musty smell and swiped a finger along a surface, examining the dust on it. If it had not been for the sawdust, he might have believed the shop had been a fantasy all along.

He looked over to the counter and a ghostly white figure sat upon it.

He hurried to it, alone in the empty shop. 'The Kaminjo tree,' he breathed. He reached to touch it, to cradle it, yet as soon as his finger came into contact, a surge of burning energy coursed through his blood. His vision went black, but he remained as bereft of any movement as the carving. A mixture of itching and burning crossed his calf, and he desperately wanted to scratch it, but his muscles refused to move.

Novo Maxia, you came back.

What's happening?

I have left you this. We wished it to be a gift.

But it burns, he cried out in his mind. He sensed agreement.

Any thief who touched it would already be dead. The Kaminjo tree is not the gift, but it is that which is stored within. The wood it is carved from can store a significant amount of energy—more than any other material. It is this which you are experiencing now.

You-you've gifted me energy?

Confirmation floated from the crocodile. *You will need it if you are to survive your journey, Novo Maxia. Fate's path is uneven where no path yet exists. Perhaps Fate will offer you an easy path to forge, though rarely are things as easy as such. Now, I suggest you stop trespassing before the guard catch you again.*

But where are you? Where did you go? Why did you leave?

We are not ones to linger. Fate leads us elsewhere, and our time in Corazin has come to its end. We will meet again, Novo Maxia. Until then.

The connection was severed, and Eder was left panting, feeling energy course through his veins. He felt alive, rested. He shifted, and felt no twinge from his leg. He tested his weight on it, then pulled his trouser leg up and the bandage aside. He felt for the wound there, where it had burned and itched, but it was gone.

All that remained was smooth skin. He marvelled at it. *Truly, there is much I do not know about magic.*

I concur, the woman said, echoing in his mind. He resisted the urge to roll his eyes. *Your crocodile friend is an interesting companion—one whom I would trust deeply. You have much to learn, Setter. Come to me. We await, as does your tuition.* With the thought, an image flashed in his mind. It was a small camp atop a hill, and with it came the knowledge of how to get there.

A pouch sat beside the carving and he slipped it within, carefully tying a knot about the top and placing it at the top of his rucksack. He left the shop, and breathed in the morning air. He could smell smoke, but as he bounced on the balls of his feet, he felt positive. Setting off at a run, he made his way north.

He had overtaken Serana at some point during the journey across the city, and he waited for her beyond the northern gate. The main gate was closed, the portcullis lowered, but he found a door to the guard's room, and below, a cellar that led underground. Unlike the tunnels around the palace, this one was a single, straight line, one with three doors: one at each end, and one in the middle. Eder unlocked each one, the doors squealing from disuse. He left them open for Serana to follow, then crept out into a forest copse. There he waited, not spying any tracks or sign that anyone had come that way for many seasons.

Serana appeared shortly after, and after a moment's surprise, she nodded to him and continued their journey. They followed the treeline, climbing and descending the rolling hills that stretched away from Corazin. Gradually the hillocks rose higher into the foothills to become the O'Pasos. She had commented on his leg, but he had feigned not knowing what she spoke of, finding some humour in it. His heart felt lighter than it had for some time, and as they rose higher, the plains stretched out below. Eder took a moment to stare, but Serana kept him moving.

Just as the morning light was beginning to dissipate across the land, they heard the nicker of a horse. As they breached the brow of the hill, they came upon a small group sat beneath a shelter of trees. They looked up as the pair approached.

A withered man with bright eyes climbed to his feet and embraced Serana, wishing her his condolences. He shook Eder's hand next. 'A strong young lad. Perhaps when you aren't training with your mind you'll learn to train your muscles, eh?' He gave Eder a wink.

The woman who had been sat next to the man, who Eder presumed was Kerrick, ignored Serana and came to Eder first. At first, he was shocked at her rudeness, but Serana seemed to take no offense, instead waiting calmly for her to finish her introduction to Eder.

'Greetings, Eder,' she said, her voice warm. 'It is good to finally meet you in person. I must say, you have impressed me as I have followed your journey. I have watched you for longer than you know, but it is a pleasure to meet you at last. My name is Alyce. I am to be your master.'

'It is an honour to meet you,' he said, bowing.

She smiled. 'You need not bow, Eder. Whilst I may be your master, I am not your lord. You will respect me and do as I ask. You will trust in my teachings and attempt no more than I teach you. Beyond that, I ask little else, as I will ask of you no more than I would expect a friend to do for me. Do you understand?'

He nodded, and she bowed her head, dismissing him. Alyce stepped to Serana. 'I am sorry for those you lost. Trust that your son's spirit is safe and his journey along Fate's path may near its end.'

'Thank you, Maxia.'

Another woman was there, whom Serana greeted with a warm embrace. She was a round woman, and their mutual silence told Eder that their bond was old and enduring. Kerrick quickly gathered a horse's reins and offered them to Serana once the women had parted. She held her hand to the horse's jaw as it huffed its satisfaction. 'There is a long journey ahead, Áxil. There won't be a stable for a long while.'

'And that's just how he'll like it,' Kerrick said, before turning to Eder. 'Apologies, lad. I had not known you were joining us until Alyce approached me. Laila here will take the spare horse. I would have found you a horse, too.'

'It's okay, Kerrick.' Alyce said, already mounted. 'He will ride with me. There are some lessons he can learn on horseback.' The man nodded and lifted himself into his own saddle as Eder joined her. Alyce walked her horse to the top of the hill, looking out across the plains and the forest below. Corazin was a black smudge in the land. Dark plumes rose into the morning sky, blemishing the orange sunrise and souring the delicate clouds. Fires still burned, and Eder thought of Trast, hoping the trader was safe.

Alyce gave a gentle pull at her reins, and the horse turned, leaving Corazin behind. Ahead, the Hackles rose high and jagged, but their journey along the O'Pasos seemed at least better than over the peaks. And beyond those?

'Duna,' Alyce said, guessing Eder's thoughts. 'There is a mountain road, but it is not an easy journey, even in the summer.'

Eder nodded, but only excitement fluttered in his chest. He was keen to be off, to head into the mountains and in a direction that finally felt right. *This is where I am meant to go,* he told himself. Here, he would leave a part of him behind, of that he was sure. If he ever returned, he would not be the same boy that set forth into the mountains.

The future is a mysterious place, Novo Maxia. Tread carefully, and tread wisely, for it is in your steps that all must follow.

Acknowledgements

Writing is often a lonely process, and in many ways, this makes the support and encouragement all the more valuable.

Firstly, thank you to my parents, for your unwavering support in every aspect of my life; perhaps without the bedtime stories and the well-stocked bookshelves, this addition would never have come to be.

Thank you to my brothers, for your ability to make me laugh when I need it most.

Thank you to Sian, for waving your flag since the first day I met you, and refusing to put it down since.

Thank you to Harry, for helping me contemplate the questions that no one else could.

Thank you to my friends, for being the necessary distractions I needed when I never knew I did.

Thank you to the lecturers at De Montfort University, for your wisdom, patience, and most importantly, your time.

May your path be true and your journey clear.

About The Author

Dominic once swore to never write fantasy, certain that situating his own writing alongside works that he admires, such as *The Inheritance Cycle,* by Christopher Paolini, and *The Farseer Trilogy,* by Robin Hobb, would be insult to both. Yet, sometimes you are looking for an adventure that can be written by no one but yourself.

Dominic is an undergraduate student at De Montfort University, studying English Language and Creative Writing. With the sun setting on his days as an undergraduate, he is looking towards the horizon, hoping that somewhere in the not-so-distant future, a career working with books and other writers awaits.

You can follow him on Twitter at: @dominic_gilmour
Or on his website at:
https://domincgilmour.wordpress.com

Printed in Poland
by Amazon Fulfillment
Poland Sp. z o.o., Wrocław